94
1 1
95
1 1
96
1 1 1

Toby Scudder, Ultimate Warrior

DAVID GIFALDI

CLARION BOOKS ▫ NEW YORK

Clarion Books
a Houghton Mifflin Company imprint
215 Park Avenue South, New York, NY 10003
Text copyright © 1993 by David Gifaldi

Printed in the U.S.A.

Library of Congress Cataloging-in-Publication Data
Gifaldi, David.
  Toby Scudder, ultimate warrior / by David Gifaldi.
    p. cm.
  Summary: Priding himself on not doing homework and on never losing a fight, Toby starts sixth grade planning to rule the school but sixth grade has some definite surprises in store for him.
  ISBN 0-395-66400-4
  [1. Behavior—Fiction. 2. Self-esteem—Fiction. 3. Schools—Fiction.] I. Title.
PZ7.G6325To 1993
[Fic]—dc20   92-39532
                                                                  CIP
                                                                   AC

AGM 10 9 8 7 6 5 4 3 2 1

For the Toby Scudders out there
And for their teachers

Toby Scudder, Ultimate Warrior

ONE

Toby Scudder, sixth grader, was in a hurry. A person could never be too early for the first day of school. There was territory to claim. New faces to check out. Summer gossip to swap.

Stopping at the corner, Toby plucked the metal spiral of his new five-subject notebook as a bus full of high schoolers passed. A tall, geeky-looking kid in the back of the bus made a face out the window, mouth opening wide and eyes bulging as if to scare Toby. Toby only smirked, thinking how he could take the skinny kid hands down . . . make him cry "Uncle" right there on the corner. When the bus turned, Toby heard the *click-click* of the kid's window as it was lowered. Then: "Hey, blubber gut!"

Toby raised his fist, his middle finger pronging high and straight. Satisfaction swept over him as he caught first the surprise, then the anger on the kid's face before the bus rushed away.

For half a block, Toby pictured himself and the kid fighting it out. Each fantasy ended with Toby forcing the kid's face into the ground and yelling, "Blubber *what?* Blubber *what?*" Passing the Texaco, Toby took a deep breath, the spring suddenly returning to his step. He didn't want any geeky high-school freshman ruining the start of what was sure to be his best year ever. *Top of the Heap. King of the School. The Year of Tobias Michael Scudder.*

Toby liked putting titles to things. Liked seeing bold headlines and newsflashes in his head. The headlines he saw just then were accompanied by pictures of kids scurrying to do his bidding. Teachers wringing their hands. Crowds parting in the halls. *It's him! It's Toby! Make way! Make way!*

Respect. What was that song? "R-E-S-P-E-C-T." No matter how you cut it, Toby had it.

Reaching into the cargo pocket of his new camouflage pants, Toby grabbed a handful of Screaming Yellow Zonkers. As he crunched, waves of sugary sweetness filled his mouth. He popped in another handful. Even breakfast tasted better this morning.

At Leo's, Toby swallowed the last of the Zonkers and finger whistled.

Leo bolted out his door with a sack lunch dangling from his hand. "Sixth grade rules!" he shouted.

"Got that right," Toby said. "Hey, cool shirt."

Leo puffed his chest wide so Toby could get a good look. An orange-colored Pluto dog covered most of the

T-shirt. The thick, black letters below spelled, *I'm Pluto . . . You Must Be Goofy!*

"Some hippie guy was selling them near where my uncle lives in California," Leo said. "The guy has to keep moving his stuff on account of the Disneyland people are out to get him."

They turned off Thirty-eighth Street and onto Alameda, then cut through the park that backed into the school's playground.

"The way I see it," Leo said, "only David Ferraro would be dumb enough to fight you this year, and I heard he moved."

"I'll take care of him if he's there," Toby answered.

"Don't hurt him too bad," Leo said with a laugh.

Toby laughed too. He liked Leo. Leo was *bad*. Leo had moved to Vancouver from Portland in the middle of last year. On his first day at Broughton Elementary, Leo had used a whole dispenser of paper towels to stuff up the toilets in the boys' bathroom. Toby had been the only witness. He'd thought it was a gutsy move for a short kid with glasses. Although neither boy had come right out and said it, it was clear there was a secret agreement between them. Toby never made fun of Leo's height. And Leo never dared mention Toby's weight.

Reaching the school grounds, Toby yelled toward a group of fifth-grade boys standing near the bike rack. "Hey, Gleason! Does your mother know you're a sissy?"

Kirk Gleason's face turned the color of his new red hightops. "No," he blustered. "I mean, yes . . . I mean—"

Toby watched to see if any of the other fifth-grade boys was going to start something. When no one did, he and Leo high fived it and sauntered over to where a bunch of sixth-grade girls stood in front of the class lists taped to the door.

"He's new," Melissa was saying.

"And cute," Veronica said. "My mother met him."

"Who's new?" Toby asked.

"Our *teacher*," Veronica replied in a tone that let Toby know she was relating information that any moron should have known. Ever since Veronica's mom had been elected president of the Broughton PTA, Veronica had become even more of a know-it-all than she'd been before. Toby looked at the huge binder and the stack of notebooks Veronica had cradled in her arms. He thought she had enough notebooks to start a store. He also thought her fresh perm made her look like a poodle.

"Mrs. *Crestfield* is taking a *year* off to be with her husband in *China*," Veronica added. "Her husband found out he'd be teaching there just last week. He's a *professor*, don't ya know? Mr. Fenning is her replacement."

"Wonder if he's mean," Josie said.

"Probably," Melissa said. "Most guy teachers are. Mean . . . and lean." She pumped her eyebrows twice as if what she'd said was a secret, girls-only kind of thing.

Josie snickered. "A lean, mean loving machine."

All three girls burst out laughing.

Toby pretended the hair over his forehead was bothering him. He swished his head from side to side real quick, hoping the girls would notice how he'd let the back grow out. He wondered if any of the girls thought he could be a loving machine. He wasn't lean, he knew that. But neither was Macho Man Randy Savage or Ultimate Warrior, or any of the big-time wrestlers, for that matter. They were big and muscled. Like Toby. Well, maybe a little more muscled. But they were big. And women went crazy for them. All you had to do was watch a match or two on TV, and you could see how the women in the audience screamed like they'd faint dead away if one of the big guys asked them out for a date. Toby drew in a breath and held it, his shoulders squaring, his new double-zero football jersey filling out.

"All I know," he said when he had to breathe again, "is no new teacher's gonna ruin this year for us. We'll show this Fenning guy what's what. We're sixth graders, right?"

Leo slapped Toby's upraised hand. "Yeah," he said. "Sixth grade rules!"

Veronica, Melissa, and Josie took up the chant. Soon the group had swelled, every sixth grader in earshot coming over. Toby pumped his arm out and back to keep the beat. The others followed suit, hands fisted. The two staff assistants monitoring the playground shook their heads and appeared to sigh as the chanting grew louder. It gave Toby a good feeling to see the kids from all the other classes watching in awe.

"Sixth grade rules! Sixth grade rules! Sixth grade rules!"

And I rule the sixth grade, Toby told himself. The thought made him work his arm faster, the others following, their voices quickening. The sound became deafening.

Yep. It was going to be a great year.

TWO

Room 15 smelled of fresh paint and new books. "Good morning," Mr. Fenning said over and over. "Find the desk with your name and make yourself at home."

Toby groaned. "We can't even sit where we want. What is this?" he told Leo. He found his desk in the middle of the fourth row and threw his notebook on top. Since the names were in alphabetical order, he and Leo found *Leo Betenstein* taped to the last desk in row 1, nearest to the sink and drinking fountain.

"Not bad," Toby said. "Looks like I'll be getting thirsty a lot."

"Yeah!" Leo said. "You can tell him you have a disease . . . and if you don't get enough water, you'll dry up and have to be rushed to the hospital."

"And that I got to pee a lot, too," Toby said. "See . . . I need the water, but it just runs out as soon as I put it in." He laughed.

When the second bell sounded, Mr. Fenning asked everyone to be seated and to bear with him while he called roll. Toby was glad to see he was sitting across from Josie. Josie didn't look all that pleased. But Toby thought he might be able to win her over. After all, Josie liked to laugh. She was almost the cutest girl in the class, too. The ultimate cutest was Joelle Nesbitt, who never laughed and who hadn't said more than ten words in all the time she'd been at Broughton.

Toby made a quick eye sweep of the room, looking for Joelle. He was surprised to see a new boy sitting in the front of the last row near the pencil sharpener. The kid didn't look that tough. He was tall and had a little muscle. But not too much. Plus he looked kind of nerdy with his hair cut so short.

Toby couldn't see any other new faces. Except—

"Luanne Davidson," Mr. Fenning called just then.

The new girl Toby had zeroed in on raised her hand.

"Welcome to Broughton," Mr. Fenning said. "You and I are both new to this class." He looked toward the pencil sharpener. "So's Jeremy."

Luanne's smile looked pained. The blood rushed to her face. Toby had to admit she looked pretty cool. She wore jeans and a shirt painted with crazy-looking coyotes. The coyotes sat in a row on their haunches, baying at an orange moon that hung there in the middle of . . .

Toby turned suddenly to get Leo's attention. He

used both hands to make a curving motion over his chest.

Leo mouthed back that he couldn't see. Toby did a Groucho Marx thing with his eyes, causing Leo to laugh. When Toby looked back, Luanne had turned to face a poster of reptiles on the wall near her desk. Pulling his name card from the front of his desk, Toby crossed out *Tobias*. Wrote *Toby*. Then added *Ultimate Warrior* on the bottom before sticking the card back in place. He hoped Luanne would notice his new card when she finished reading the reptile poster.

"Tobias Michael Scudder."

"Toby," Toby said. "Call me Toby. My goldfish do."

Laughter.

Mr. Fennning pressed his lips together and nodded. He looked neither lean nor mean. He was of medium height and build and had a dark mustache. His red suspenders made bright splashes over a crisp, fresh-from-the-laundry pinstripe shirt.

"Toby it is, then," he said. His voice was full of the usual first-day optimism. Toby was sure the man's confidence would be lowered more than a notch before the end of the day.

"Like your suspenders," Toby said.

The snickers came at once from every direction. Toby held his gaze on the teacher.

"Thank you," Mr. Fenning said. "This is a first for me. Actually two firsts. First time teaching sixth grade. And first time wearing suspenders.

"But neither is as fascinating as those amazing fish of yours," he added. "You mean they talk? They call you Toby?"

"Not really," Toby said. "They don't actually talk. Not in the regular way. They're ventriloquists. And I can read lips."

More laughter. Toby could feel himself sweating, but he always sweated when he was matching wits with someone. And he was pretty sure that's what he and Mr. Fenning were doing. Sparring. Like boxers do. Checking each other out. Toby looked quickly at the new girl. Luanne had finished learning about the life cycle of the king snake. She was looking Toby's way, her complexion back to its regular color.

"And what do you call them, these goldfish of yours?" Mr. Fenning asked.

His voice sounded normal, not strained like a guy on the edge of losing his cool. Besides, Toby always knew when an adult was going to blow a gasket. All you had to do was check out the neck. When the muscles tightened hard so you could see ropy veins and stuff, you could usually count on seeing an explosion any second.

There were no ropy veins around Mr. Fenning's neck. In fact, he seemed to be enjoying himself. He had his thumbs stuck under his suspenders and looked sort of like some old-time politician in a made-for-TV movie.

"Fish," Toby said. "They're fish, so I call them fish.

That way they don't get confused. I mean, if I called them cats or dogs . . . what then?"

Mr. Fenning laughed. "Good point. Wouldn't want to confuse the little critters, would we?"

"He's lying!" The shrill voice made Toby's ears jump. He jerked around to see.

"His fish are called some stupid *wrestling* names," Veronica went on. "Don't ya know he's just pulling your leg?"

If a meat grinder had been handy, Toby would have gotten up, lifted Veronica off her seat, and made some know-it-all sausage.

"We're just getting to know one another," Mr. Fenning said. "That's all. Nothing life and death about it. I can enjoy a good fib as well as the next man. But how do you know Toby didn't change his fishes' names just this morning . . . that is, if they had been named something different in the first place? Hard to tell, isn't it"—he craned his neck to see her name card— "Veronica?"

Veronica sniffed the air. "A lie is a lie!" she said.

"Dry up," Toby said.

"I think this has gone far enough," Mr. Fenning said. "We want to get off on a good footing. Might as well be courteous to one another. We're here for the duration, aren't we?"

Most everybody nodded.

"Aren't we?"

Toby forced himself to nod. Mr. Fenning looked past Toby to Veronica. Veronica must have nodded, too, because the teacher smiled as if the discussion were over.

"Good, then let's get started. I want everyone to take out a sheet of paper and to write as much as you can on a subject near and dear to you: Yourself!" He strode up to the board and scrawled *About Me* across two whole panels. "That's our title—now let's go at it."

There was a din of clicks from the opening and closing of ring binders, and a rash of rippings as pages were torn from spiral notebooks.

"I think I forgot how to write," somebody said.

"My mind hasn't been turned back on yet," someone else said.

"It will, of course," Mr. Fenning said in a commanding voice, "be absolutely quiet." He took a sign that said *Shhhh! . . . Brains at Work* from his desk and taped it to the board.

Toby thought the guy had a lot of nerve, having them work when they'd barely been in the room for ten minutes. And he especially didn't like the way everyone, including Leo and Josie and the new coyote girl, was already writing as if you had to do whatever he said. Like he was the boss or something.

With a resounding rip, Toby tore off a sheet of paper. *About Me*, he scribbled in the center.

My name is Toby. My full name is Tobias Michael Scudder. I have two fish, one mother, one half-brother, one half-sister, and one father who flew the coop. Pretty boring. About as boring as this assignment!!!

Toby slammed down his pencil. Then he picked it up again and went to the pencil sharpener. The new kid was writing. Toby reached for the sharpener, bumping the kid's desk with his hip. "Oops!" he said. The kid shrugged, like it didn't matter, and went back to writing. Toby sharpened his pencil to a fine point, then started back, giving the desk another bump on the way.

Reaching his own desk, Toby decided a drink would be just the thing. He made a move toward the back of the room. Mr. Fenning called his name. "Please stay seated till we're all finished," the teacher said.

"But I'm thirsty."

Mr. Fenning shook his head, his pen pointing to Toby's desk.

Toby sat down, grumbling under his breath about schools and prisons being one and the same. He drummed his fingers on the desk, trying to drown out the scratching sounds of all the writing around him. Toby hated writing and pretty much everything else about school, except for P.E. and recesses and lunch and the other fun stuff. But the work itself . . . Toby thought they could shove all that.

"I'm writing about our vacation to Alaska this summer," Josie whispered to Toby as she started her second page.

Toby shrugged like he didn't think it was such a whoop-de-doo. But he knew Alaska was a pretty big deal. Just as California had been a big deal for Leo. Toby didn't even want to start thinking about his own summer. The weekend camping trip with Mr. Fitness had been the pits. And his stay with Aunt Rhonda and Uncle Kevin and the boys had been even more of a bust.

Searching the inside of his desk for something to do, Toby was pleased to find a rubber band stuck among a few old crayon pieces way in the back. He pulled the band a couple of times to test its strength, then ripped off a chunk of eraser from his pencil. He would have liked to fire a shot at Leo just for laughs, but Leo was behind him and Toby wanted to stay out of trouble for as long as possible this year. His mother had already told him that he'd best watch himself because she was tired of being called in to hear the teachers bellyache about his behavior.

Toby armed the band with the eraser piece and pulled it taut. He released his fingers, Michael Adams his target. The eraser flew past Michael's bent head and reached the open doorway just as the doorway became filled with a beige wool suit. Toby wouldn't have thought anything about an eraser flicking off the lapel of an ordinary beige wool suit. But this suit happened to belong to Mrs. Janet Hawkins, Broughton's principal.

Wincing, Toby quickly palmed the rubber band.

Mrs. Hawkins swept in, smiling. "I need your

count," she told Mr. Fenning softly, as if not wanting to disturb the learning that was going on.

Attendance folder in hand, Mrs. Hawkins spread her smile out over the classroom. "Good morning," she mouthed to those who had looked up. Then, smile dissolving, she crooked a finger at Toby.

"May I see Tobias for a moment?" she asked the teacher.

Mr. Fenning nodded.

Toby got up. The stupid eraser hadn't been meant for her. Mrs. Hawkins would let him have it, all right. But most likely he'd end up with a warning and a lot of blah-blah-blah about having a good year.

As he pulled himself toward the door, Toby had a newsflash.

Tobias Michael Scudder, age 12, took out the principal of his school today with a deadly plug of eraser taken from the top of a thoroughly innocent No. 2 pencil. Asked by reporters if he was sorry for his actions, Tobias said: "Who gives a rip? . . . I've already erased it from my mind!"

THREE

Out in the hall, Mrs. Hawkins did her thing.

"I'm not putting up with any nonsense this year," she said. "It's up to you. You're in control of your own destiny around here. Be a responsible citizen, and all will go right for you. Break the rules, and you'll have to pay the price. Am I getting through?"

Toby acknowledged that she was getting through.

"This is a fresh year. You've had some problems in school in the past, but everything starts anew today. Get it?"

Toby got it. What he didn't get was why Mrs. Hawkins wore such awful perfume, and why her two-tone hair (brown and copper) looked so much like the fur of some small mammal. As she droned on about making one's own bed and sleeping in it, Toby saw first a beaver, then a fox, and finally a weasel atop the woman's skull. Each animal he saw had thick brown-

and-copper fur—pouffed high and stiff, as if the creature had run into an electric fence. He considered offering Mrs. Hawkins a free hairstyling, thinking Andrea might welcome the challenge. Now that she was in her fourth month of study at the Vancouver Hair College, his half-sister Andrea was always looking for people to practice on.

". . . I said, you may return to class now."

She smiled. It was the same smile she'd used last year when she'd suspended Toby just because he'd socked Brian Loper in the stomach after Brian called him a cheater during a recess football game. Toby didn't let little maggots like Brian call him a cheater, even if he did sometimes bend the rules. Everyone bent the rules. Especially adults. Mrs. Hawkins bent the rules by having favorite students and favorite families. Toby's mom bent the rules by telling Toby she'd beat him silly if he ever started drinking, then coming home at three in the morning, stumbling and giggling, with some jerk of a guy she always introduced the next morning as her "new friend."

"Toby?"

He decided Mrs. Hawkins didn't deserve a hair make-over after all. Let her walk around with a weasel on her head.

□　□　□

Toby could hear his stomach making "Feed me" noises when lunchtime rolled around. He checked all his pockets, front and back, but came up empty. Since his mother worked nights, she usually slept in, and Toby had forgotten to ask her for money before she'd left for work yesterday. Once his mother filled out the free-lunch form that was in the take-home packet on his desk, Toby would be assured a lousy cafeteria lunch for the rest of the year. But today he'd have to wait till he got home to chow down.

The cafeteria was noisy and full of teachers making sure everything went smoothly the first day.

"You're not eating," Mr. Fenning said, stopping in his tour of the sixth-grade tables.

"Not hungry," Toby said.

"I know they don't allow charges, but if it's a question of money, I could cover you till tomorrow."

"Not hungry," Toby said. He looked over at Leo, forcing his eyeballs as high as they'd go under their lids.

Leo laughed.

"What's this I hear about the cook whipping up a sandwich for anyone who doesn't have a lunch?" Mr. Fenning said.

"Dried-out peanut butter on stale bread?" Toby scoffed. "No thanks."

"Remember David Ferraro last year?" Leo said, looking at Toby but wanting Mr. Fenning to hear. "David couldn't get his mouth open for two days after eating one of *her* sandwiches." Leo cast a glance toward the cook, who was busy plopping corn dogs onto trays as students filed down the lunch line. "She does it on purpose. So people won't forget their money or cold lunches."

Mr. Fenning couldn't quite hide his smile. "Suit yourself, then," he said before moving off.

The sixth-grade tables were lined up nearest the windows. Toby sat at the end of the last table, Leo opposite him. Jake Curanza, Chris Whiting, and Denny Sasser sat nearby, nibbling corn dogs. Craig Andretti and Shawn Reynolds were already into their Pudding Pops. A few boys down from Shawn sat Brian Loper and the new kid. Then the girls began.

"Want some?" Leo said, offering Toby half his tuna-fish sandwich.

Toby made a face, waving the sandwich off. "That Fenning's a jerk," he said. "Never heard of a teacher assigning work the first day."

"Teachers always think they're gods," Leo said. He took a bite of tuna sandwich, his nose crinkling. "This stuff stinks, don't it?"

"Like Mrs. Hawkins' feet," Toby said.

Jake and Chris and Denny laughed along with Leo. Toby was glad he'd thought of the joke so quickly.

Leo pulled out some vanilla wafers from his lunch bag before shoving the stinky sandwich back inside. He stuffed three wafers into his mouth and gave Toby the other three. Then he raised his fist. There was a thump.

"Oh, gross!" Jake said, pointing to where some of the smashed tuna was oozing out a corner of the lunch bag.

Toby laughed. He used his own fist to give the bag another bash. By now everyone, including the girls, had been alerted to the tuna clobbering, and Toby's bash was followed by an echoing chorus of "Grrrooooosss!"

Raising his fist again, Toby let it drop even harder. *Thunk.* A new, higher-pitched round of "Yuck" and "Ick" and "Double gross" came from both boys and girls.

"Hey, Loper . . . catch!" Toby said, flicking the now thoroughly dampened bag and its contents Frisbee style down the table. Screams and laughter erupted as everyone ducked, the bag spinning gobs of tuna. Brian Loper backed away so quickly in his chair that he toppled over, his tray following behind him with a clatter. The bag came to a sudden splatting halt against the new kid's tray, which the kid had quickly raised in self-defense. The laughter came louder.

Red-faced but laughing, the new kid picked up the squashed bag and flung it back down the table from where it had come. Toby was still in mid chuckle when he was hit square in the chest, the bag exploding its contents over his new shirt.

"You buttwipe!" Toby called down.

"Takes one to know one!" the kid shot back.

Toby's anger was like a flame roaring up after being fed gasoline. He could feel his neck muscles tighten . . . knew ropy veins and stuff were showing.

Blindly, Toby wheeled from the table and rushed for the new kid.

"TOBIAS! TOBIAS SCUDDER!"

The fire that was Toby stopped its forward movement and flamed in place. Toby was close enough to the new kid to see the hard emotion glinting in his eyes.

"TOBIAS!"

At first Toby didn't recognize the voice. So many teachers and staff assistants had made beelines for the sixth-grade tables, that it could've been anyone. But then the realization sank in.

"TOBIAS!" Mrs. Hawkins said. "I'll see you in my office at once!

"And you, young man . . . what's your name?"

The new kid kept his eyes on Toby, fists clenched.

"Jeremy," he said.

"I'll see you, too, Jeremy."

Toby felt the anger heat *whoosh* again. The boy was no longer *the new kid* to him. He was *Jeremy*. He had a name like any challenger would. *Ultimate Warrior versus The Barbarian*. The headline flashed across Toby's mind. He couldn't tell if Jeremy was scared or just embarrassed at getting caught by the principal. But to Toby it didn't much matter. The only thing that mattered was that Jeremy was standing there with his shoulders back, fists clenched. Anybody could see it was a challenge. A challenge that would have to be met, regardless of Mrs. Hawkins or

Mr. Fenning or his mother or anyone. This was Toby's year, after all. And no new kid was going to take away from him what was rightfully his.

□   □   □

Toby sat in the health room all through lunch recess. Mrs. Hawkins waited till the bell rang before calling him into her office. She'd already talked to Jeremy and a number of witnesses. *Witnesses.* That's what she called them.

"You threw the bag," she said after Toby had given his version. "Threw it first, in fact. Here's the phone. Call your mother and let her know that you've had two slip-ups already. Then let me talk to her."

"She's not home," Toby said.

"Doesn't she still work at the bowling alley?"

He studied the big wall calendar that had been decorated with a cutout old-fashioned schoolhouse and letters spelling *Welcome Back.*

"She works evenings and nights, doesn't she?"

"She had a doctor's appointment," Toby said, his toes curling tight in his shoes.

Mrs. Hawkins shoved the phone over. "Call!"

Toby lifted the receiver. He dialed and waited. He heard his mother's voice. Muttered that he was in trouble. Then held the phone away from his ear as she let loose. Embarrassed that Mrs. Hawkins could hear, he put the receiver back—holding it tight to his ear, mumbling "Yes" and "No" and "I will."

He got back to class in the middle of a video on the

five senses. After Mr. Fenning had discussed the video, it was pretty much time to get everything ready to go.

"I'd like to see you for a minute," Mr. Fenning told Toby when the bell rang.

"I'll wait for you outside," Leo said, coming up to Toby's desk. "Everybody thinks you and Jeremy are gonna fight after school."

"Leo . . ." Mr. Fenning said. "Good-*bye*. There'll be no fights. Please take your things and *go*."

"You don't have to get nasty over it," Leo said. He shot Toby a smile.

Toby slapped him five. Then Leo left, and Toby put on his sorry look for Mr. Fenning, preparing himself for the lecture he knew was coming. He *was* sorry, of course. Sorry he'd gotten caught and that his mother would be all over him. He also thought Mr. Fenning must be something of a fool not to realize that there would have to be a fight. Not today, of course. Maybe not for a week or two or more. But it was a sure thing. You could bet on it.

FOUR

"I just can't stop thinking about it," Leo said on the way home from school. "I mean, all those bikini-clad babes. Whole beaches just packed full of nearly naked girls!"

Since returning from his trip, Leo had told Toby about California at least a hundred times. Toby wondered if he'd ever get tired of hearing the story. He doubted it. Although he'd been born in Arizona, Toby hadn't been anyplace farther than Seattle since he'd moved to Washington when he was five. Just the name *California* sounded warm and happy and exotic. Toby thought bikini-clad babes would be an extra bonus.

When they neared Leo's apartment, Leo asked Toby what he wanted to do.

"I've gotta check in first," Toby said. "Mom wants to chew me out." He didn't say anything about how embarrassed he'd been knowing Mrs. Hawkins had heard his mother have a cow over the phone.

"I'll call you when she leaves for work," Toby said. "Then you can bring the football over and we can throw it around."

Leo split off, and Toby walked the rest of the way by himself, checking every passing bus for the high-schooler he'd given the finger to. He thought there was a slight possibility his mom had already left for work. If so, he'd be sure to find a note. Mrs. Scudder was good at leaving angry notes about how Toby or Gordon or Andrea was going to be the death of her. Well, not Andrea anymore, now that she'd moved into her own place. Toby thought a note would be a zillion times better than seeing his mother in person if she was still mad.

"No such luck," he muttered when he reached the house. The car was still in the driveway, the back door open. Through the screen he could hear the hair dryer running in the bathroom.

"Hi, Mom!" he yelled as happily as he could. "Mom? . . . I'm home."

Mrs. Scudder ducked into the kitchen, the hair dryer whining, her long hair fluttering outward with the force of air. She pointed with her free hand for Toby to stay put, then swung her head back to the bathroom mirror.

Toby grabbed an apple from the fridge and bit into it. He looked at the white of the apple where he'd bitten and thought about putting a hunk of peanut butter there for his next bite. But his mother was always on him for eating too much peanut butter, so he resisted.

He'd taken three bites (he could usually finish even a large apple in four) when the hair dryer clicked dead and his mother came out, brushing her still-damp hair with short, quick strokes.

"Already? The first day? What did I tell you? What did you promise me?"

Toby tried to swallow, but the last bite he'd taken was a doozie, and he had to speak through half-chewed apple.

"Exactly," she said. "You promised this was going to be your best year ever. That's what you said. You promised. And look. First day, and I get a phone call." Her voice imitated his. " 'Mom . . . It's me, Toby. I got in trouble. . . .' "

She threw up her hands. "And I had to talk to that *woman* again. You know how she ticks me off with her *Now, Mrs. Scudder* this and *Mrs. Scudder* that in that voice of hers! So once again I had to make excuses. Tell her it won't happen again. First day!"

She went back to brushing, working the other side, her face grimacing as the brush fought its way through. She had on her new black jeans and a pink sweatshirt with the sleeves cut off. After a final flurry of strokes, she used a bare foot to slide her sandals out from beneath the table and slipped them on.

Toby thought about asking her to measure against

him back to back. He was sure he had passed her since the last time. Bodywise, height was about all Toby and his mom had in common. Mrs. Scudder was thin. And other than a tiny mole to one side of her chin, she was zitless. Toby and Leo often talked about how totally unfair it was that adults didn't get zits. They had come up with several theories, one of which was that the Oxy-10 and Clearasil people had hired a voodoo witch to put a curse on young people in order to sell their creams.

Mrs. Scudder banged the brush against her jeans a few times. "Well, you're grounded, buster," she said. She picked out a bunch of hair and rushed to deposit it in the bag under the sink. "You can call Leo and let him know right now. 'Cause except for school, you are housebound for the next three days."

Toby stopped chewing and swallowed what was in his mouth, his throat stretching to accommodate.

"Three days!" he said. "Just 'cause some twerp threw a smashed tuna sandwich at me?"

"I'll call you every hour on the hour. You miss my call even once, and you won't see the sky for a lot longer than three days. Is that clear?"

In the past Toby had been able to cut the length of his groundings by saying how being housebound was cruel and unusual punishment for a kid like him. He never mentioned his weight, but the message always got through. "I'll do whatever else you want," he'd say. "But, Mom, I *need* to get out and run around."

"And don't worry about getting exercise," she shot

as if reading his mind. She grabbed the notepad from the catch-all basket on the counter. "You'll have plenty to do. Here's a list. Start with number one and check off as you go. What'd you eat for lunch?"

"Nothing."

"I bought some frozen dinners. And there's macaroni and cheese or soup if you want. And fruit." She looked at the core he was still holding. "You can eat as much fruit as you want. Gordon will be getting off work early now that school has started. He should be home by nine-thirty. . . . He'd better be," she added. "And Andrea might stop over with my Avon stuff."

She bit the inside of her cheek as if trying to remember something else. When her gaze caught the clock above the stove, she shrieked, "Now, look what time it is! The new league starts tonight. It'll be a zoo. I should be there already." She shoved the job list at him. "Gimme a kiss 'bye."

He sighed and allowed her to give him a peck on the cheek. The fresh perfume stung his nose.

"And don't let Andrea touch your hair. It looks great just the way it is. I know she's hunting for guinea pigs. Tell her no, okay?"

He nodded. She wended her way around the ironing board and into the front room, where she grabbed her purse from the sofa. In a moment the car roared to life in the driveway. Toby was on the phone to Leo even before she'd backed out. "I'm a prisoner in my own house," he said.

"Heck," Leo said. "Again? Okay, no sweat. I'll be right over with the football."

Toby flung the job list on the counter. His bedroom was off the front room. He'd forgotten to lift the shade before leaving for school, and the place was like a cave. With a loud crackle and snap, the shade shot up, the light like a knife carving up the darkness. Slammer and Crusher went nuts with the sudden noise and instant light. The two fish swam tight circles in their bowl on the nightstand. Toby shook some food into the bowl. "You guys miss me?" he asked. The fish jabbed at and swallowed one morsel after the other. Toby sat on the edge of the bed and watched, fascinated as always by their quickness. Ever since he'd won the fish at last spring's school carnival, he'd wondered how fish could eat without swallowing water and filling up like water balloons. He'd even stooped low enough to ask Gordon about it.

" 'Cause they're fish, you idiot," Gordon had said. "They're built to spit out the water while they eat, like spitting out sunflower-seed shells after you take out the insides. You'll learn all about this kind of stuff when you take biology."

As much as Toby watched, he never saw evidence of Slammer or Crusher spitting out water. Plus Gordon had flunked tenth-grade biology last year, which Toby thought was another good reason not to believe him.

Watching up close now, Toby thought he'd like to

be as quick as Slammer and Crusher were. And to be able to flex his body as easily as they flexed theirs. He had a sudden picture of himself in a big tank of water, spinning perfect circles, his fins cutting this way and that. Suddenly a giant shadow moved above, and chunks of food came shooting down around him. Toby the fish jabbed and ate, jabbed and ate. He saw himself getting bigger and bigger. Fatter and fatter. Nearly filling his tank. Until he exploded, his guts pouring out, the water suddenly filled with partly digested bits of Screaming Yellow Zonkers.

Toby shuddered, his eyes refocusing on the bowl. Crusher had stopped eating. He looked out at Toby, his mouth nearly touching the glass.

"It's okay," Toby said. "Just a dream."

He wondered if fish had dreams. Dreams of being faster or slimmer or smarter, or of being some other fish altogether.

□   □   □

Later that night Toby lay on the sofa watching reruns. He sat through two *Mork and Mindy*s, one *Alf*, and one *Who's the Boss?*, and was waiting for the commercials to end so he could see his favorite, *Married . . . With Children*. Though it was dark outside, Toby didn't bother turning on the lamp. He liked the way the TV glowed blue-gray in the darkened room.

Earlier Toby and Leo had played catch out in the street. Toby had left the front door open and had turned up the ringer volume all the way so he wouldn't miss his mother's call. She called a little after six, asking if Andrea had come by and if he had any homework. "No," he'd said to both. Mrs. Scudder hadn't called again, and Toby thought it was a real waste that he hadn't agreed to Leo's suggestion to go to the Texaco Mart for a Big Burpie.

On the TV, Al Bundy, the raunchy father of *Married . . . With Children,* was planning to take the family on vacation to this hole of a motel somewhere down south where no one in his right mind would want to be. Al was trying to save money.

Mostly, what Toby liked about the show was how Al was such a moron. He liked the idea that there might be a lot of Als out there. A lot of kids with fathers like Al, and how—if you looked at it a certain way—those kids were probably a lot worse off than Toby. Sometimes Toby thought it might be lucky that his own father had flown the coop early on. He didn't want any nerdy Al-type guy slouched on the sofa with his hand stuck under his belt, ordering Toby to get him beers and stuff.

Toby lost track of what was happening on the TV. He didn't like the way his thoughts had gone. Of course his father wasn't a moron like Al. He even said his father's name out loud. "Blaine Kellogg." Just like that. Out loud right there in the dark room with the blue-gray TV glow. With a name like Blaine Kellogg, a guy couldn't be a nerd, Toby thought. And he suddenly recalled how when he once suggested that his father might be an heir to the Kellogg cereal fortune, his mother had laughed only a little.

"Well, the man did have a way with money," she'd said. "And he *was* born in Michigan." Which had been enough to make Toby think that it was possible after all. Anything was possible, Toby thought.

He made a face when he saw that the show was a two-parter, the picture suddenly freezing and "To Be Continued" splashing on the screen. He got up and took his plate and glass into the kitchen, the light making him blink when he flicked it on. He was just about finished with the dishes, the first item on his job list, when he heard a car squeal off.

Gordon rushed in, bow tie in hand, his white shirt halfway unbuttoned so that his bare chest showed through. Gordon hardly ever buttoned his shirts all the way. Once Toby had heard Gordon explaining to a girl over the phone that he kept his shirts opened because he was so hot-blooded.

"Hey, Tub," Gordon said.

"Shove it," Toby answered.

Gordon speared a Coke from the fridge. "How was your first day in the *big* sixth grade?"

"You'll never know," Toby said, balancing the not-quite-all-the-way-clean macaroni-and-cheese pot atop the already crowded drainer. "How was the BIG eleventh grade?"

"Just biding my time . . . biding my time. Two

more years and this kid is off to be all that he can be. . . . What's this?"

"It's a list—what does it look like?"

Toby watched Gordon's eyes move over the paper.

"Who's supposed to do all this?"

"Us," Toby said.

"No way, man. I've got phone calls to make."

"You better at least sweep and straighten the front room," Toby said, which was the second item on the list. "Or Mom will be mad. I did the dishes."

Gordon reached out suddenly, wrenching Toby's arm back in a hammerlock. He was taller and stronger than Toby, but Toby figured he was gaining on his half-brother fast. Toby was waiting for the day he'd feel strong enough to pop Gordon a good one. He figured that happy moment wasn't too far away.

"A mosquito," Toby said, pretending his arm didn't hurt. "Some jerky mosquito's landed on my arm."

"Buzz off," Gordon said, releasing his grip. He picked up his Coke, drained it, burped, then scowled his way to the utility closet, where he cursed as he took out the broom and dustpan.

Toby smiled and checked off Job #2.

□   □   □

Later, as he lay in bed after finishing off the box of Zonkers he'd opened for breakfast, Toby had a news-flash.

Today Mr. Blaine Kellogg, wealthy heir to the Kellogg cereal fortune, pulled up in front of 2308 Aspen Street in a red Ferrari, the keys to which he immediately handed over to a local boy—one Tobias Michael Scudder, his long-lost son. "I had no idea you were living in this dump," Mr. Kellogg said upon eyeing the Scudder residence. Tobias, age twelve, thanked his father, took the keys, and was last seen screeching doughnuts in the Broughton Elementary parking lot with a bikini-clad babe by his side.

FIVE

Mr. Fenning assigned more work in the first four days than Toby remembered any teacher assigning in a month. "He's a slave-driver," Leo said. Not that it mattered to Toby. Toby never got past the first five minutes of any assignment anyway. And homework was out of the question. Toby didn't do homework. He never had. He figured everyone had something they didn't do. He'd heard people say things like "I don't mow the lawn." Or "I don't do dishes." He'd learned over the summer that Uncle Kevin didn't do bathrooms and Aunt Rhonda didn't do cars.

Toby didn't do homework.

On Friday, Mr. Fenning gave back the first-day "About Me" papers. There was a note attached to Toby's: *I wish you had written more. Perhaps you'll want to share more about yourself some other time.*

Sure, Toby thought. *Like in a hundred million years!*

Mr. Fenning opened the front supply closet and lifted out a stack of books.

"More books?" two or three people muttered at the same time.

"Fear not," Mr. Fenning said as he set the stack on his desk. "These aren't your usual kind of books. I think you're going to like these."

"Must be sex ed!" Leo called from the back. "All right! Color photos? Or just black and white?"

"Sorry, Mr. Betenstein," the teacher answered. "Sex ed will come later. . . . I can assure you I'm not looking forward to it."

"Well, when we do get sex ed," Toby said, "do we get to have study partners?" Everyone laughed. Toby looked over at Josie and pointed as if to say *you and me.*

Josie shivered as if she'd stepped in something not so nice. She slid to the edge of her seat, away from Toby, her shoulder rising defensively. "You wish," she said.

Toby made himself belch. Not overly loud. But solid. Mr. Fenning shot him a look and Toby excused himself. "It slipped," he said. "Honest."

Mr. Fenning held up one of the books. It was a composition notebook of some kind, with a solid-blue cover, much thicker than the usual paper covers. The binding was more like that of a real book, too. On the cover was a white label with something typed on it.

"Allow me to present to you your autobiographies," Mr. Fenning said.

"Our what?"

He began passing out the books, beginning with Michael Adams in the first row, carefully setting a book on each desk. When Toby got his, he was surprised to see his name typed on the label. *MY LIFE,* the label said, *by TOBY SCUDDER.*

What followed were mostly groans. Although no one knew exactly what Mr. Fenning had up his sleeve, it was obvious from the books' blank pages that work was to play a major role.

Returning to the front of the room, Mr. Fenning explained that he didn't want to see these books in school again until the second of November.

"That's two days after Halloween for those of you on Holiday Time," he said. "That's when they're due. Until then they're to stay at home, where you will fill the pages with your own life story. Past. Present. How you feel about things. Your vision of yourself in the future. Hopes and dreams. Whatever you want."

"A diary?" someone said. "We gotta do a diary?"

"You mean we gotta write something every day from now till Halloween?" Jake Curanza said.

"How often you write is up to you," Mr. Fenning answered. "I didn't say you had to write every day. I don't expect to see an entry for every single day when you turn them in."

"You're gonna read our private stuff!" Josie gasped.

"Do we get graded?" asked Melissa.

"Can we lie?"

"I hate this kind of stuff."

Mr. Fenning put up his hands and waited till everyone had calmed down.

"Whether or not I read what you end up writing about yourself is entirely up to you. When you hand in your book, you'll write one of two things on the cover. Either *Don't Read* or *Read*. I will respect your wishes. But in order to pass this assignment, you must have written *something*. The more you write, the higher your grade. Filling half the book will net you a B. Beyond that you'll receive a B+, A−, A, or A+, depending on how much more you've written. Likewise, your score will go down from B according to how *little* you've written. When you hand the book in, if it says *Don't Read*, all I'll do is flip through just to see how much is there."

"How much do we have to have not to get an F?" Toby said.

"I hadn't even thought of that," Mr. Fenning said. "But if you must pin me down, I'd guess that the least I'd accept for a passing grade would be . . . oh . . . let's say ten pages."

"Ten pages!" Toby said.

"Front and back," Mr. Fenning said.

Toby thought the man must be nuts. He'd never written ten pages of anything in his life. Besides, he didn't *do* homework. Especially diaries or journals or auto-whatevers.

"Does that take care of the numbers stuff?" Mr. Fenning said.

"What if your life story takes *more* than one book?" Veronica asked in her exact way. "I mean, I'm pretty sure *mine* will. I've been *so* many places. Why, just this past summer I went to Washington, D.C., and traveled through *fourteen states,* including Wyoming, where we camped at Yellowstone Park. And then last *winter,* I . . ."

Toby wanted to clamp his hand over Veronica's mouth. Of course, being Veronica, she'd probably just keep on talking. Then he'd be forced to feel the vibrations of her trapped voice and the jiggle of her jaw and the heat of her breath . . . all the while looking down into her angry, know-it-all eyes. He shook his hand as if it had Veronica breath on it, a creepy feeling rising from his palm to his shoulder. He shuddered.

"You fill one book, you ask me for another" was Mr. Fenning's casual reply when Veronica finally had to stop to breathe. "Any other questions?"

"Can we start like when we were babies, just born?" Melissa asked.

"An excellent idea," Mr. Fenning said. "If you can remember back that far! If you can't remember, but you'd still like to start at the beginning, you can write what you know about yourself as a baby from pictures and stories that your parents or grandparents have related to you."

"You mean like how I always waited to pee until I was in the middle of being changed?" Leo called out. "Dad thought I had the makings of a fireman."

Everyone burst out laughing. Toby turned to Leo and gave him thumbs up.

"And on that humorous and rather wet note," Mr. Fenning said, "this discussion is officially over."

□   □   □

It rained hard Saturday. Toby spent the day cooped up inside the darkened house. His mother was in and out, running errands and carping to Toby about how he never helped her. If Leo had been around, Toby would have escaped to his house. But Leo was spending the weekend with his father in Portland.

Around suppertime Andrea burst in with Mrs. Scudder's Avon order.

"I hate this rain!" Andrea said, handing Toby her drippy umbrella before charging toward the light of the kitchen.

Toby left the TV glowing and followed her, tossing the wet umbrella onto the sofa to dry.

"Here," Andrea told her mother. "I think it's all here. The order came in late. I've been getting soaked all day trying to deliver everything. You'd think it was winter already, the way it's been coming down. What's up, Tobe?"

Toby shrugged.

"That's twenty-one seventy, Mom," Andrea said. She poured herself a cup of coffee from the Mr. Coffee. "Whatcha doin'?"

Mrs. Scudder stood at the stove, browning meatballs for the sauce she was making. "Our softball team's having its end-of-the-season potluck. Should be fun. It's at the VFW Hall. The Lanes' men's team is coming too." She turned down the burner, then fumbled through her purse for her checkbook.

"Where's Gordon?" Andrea said.

"At the grocery," Toby said. "Pretending to work. All those guys do is hang out in the back, smoking cigarettes."

"You let Gordon *smoke?*" Andrea asked.

"He'd better not be," Mrs. Scudder said.

"You guys do," Toby said. "What's the big deal?"

"The big deal is that I say no," his mother said.

"Dad called," Andrea said. "He doesn't think Gordon should be working now that school has started."

"Carl always liked being boss from afar," Mrs. Scudder said. "Did he say anything else?"

"Nope. Just that he's glad I'm sticking with the hair college. He's still afraid his money might go to waste."

"He should be worried about the money his wife spends."

Carl Scudder was Andrea and Gordon's father. He lived with his second family in Olympia. Toby liked Carl because whenever Carl came down to visit Andrea and Gordon, he usually slipped Toby a ten-dollar bill.

Toby moved to the stove. The meatballs were simmering nicely, sending up a steamy aroma of meat

and herbs. A pot of sweet-smelling tomato sauce bur-
bled on the back burner. "These need testing," Toby
said, using the fork on the stove to spear one of the
meatballs.

"Just one," his mother said. "I'm leaving you
plenty for your supper. All you'll have to do is cook
the spaghetti."

Andrea had turned her attention to Toby's hair.
"You want a tail?" she said. "I could give you a tail.
Your hair's long enough now. We could shave around
the ears some . . . maybe bring the shave lines down
to the back so they meet at the tail."

"You keep your mitts off him," Mrs. Scudder
said.

Andrea waved off the comment. "What do ya say,
Tobe?"

Toby pictured himself going to school with a
duck's tail and shave lines. He wondered what the
kids would say. "I don't know," he said. "It might
look cool."

"It's *his* head," Andrea said before Mrs. Scudder
could protest. "Let the kid do what he wants."

"He'll look like a freak!"

"No he won't—he'll look cool. Tails are the thing."

Toby had been waiting for the meatball to cool. He
now bit into it, steam rising. "I'll think about it," he
said.

□   □   □

Even with the shade down, Toby could tell that the rain had stopped. Sunlight shone through the shade's worn material. In their bowl, Slammer and Crusher faced the glow. Drowsily, Toby poured in some food flakes. "Mornin', you guys," he said.

The fish made plopping sounds as they jumped for the food. Toby liked hearing the sounds. Liked knowing the fish counted on him. And that he could count on them . . . to be there. Someone to talk to. He was proud he had proved his mother wrong. "They'll be dead in a week," Mrs. Scudder had said the night of the carnival, when Toby showed her the clear-plastic sandwich bag bulging with water, the two flashes of orange darting within. "You can't even take care of yourself."

Toby threw on his robe, glad that he'd gone to the pet store right away and talked to the clerk. "Better change your water today," he told Slammer and Crusher. "And no arguments this time."

The house always looked better with the sun coming in. The popcorn smell from last night still hung in the air. Toby tossed the sofa cushions back where they belonged, then picked up the bowl, which had a few burned kernels stuck to the bottom. Some popped kernels lay scattered on the floor around the TV, but he figured he'd get them later.

Toby always made popcorn for *Saturday Night's Main Event*. It gave him the feeling that he was actually there at ringside. Sometimes he threw his popcorn at the TV screen, just like the people in the seats threw things and booed at the wrestlers they hated. Taking the bowl to the kitchen, Toby took satisfaction in recalling how Cactus Jack had defeated Mr. Hughes.

Gordon's room was in the basement, and Toby listened at the top of the stairs to see if Gordon was awake. He hadn't heard Gordon come in last night. Nor had he heard his mother. Let the sleepyheads sleep, Toby thought. He liked being up first with the sun streaming in like this, and decided to surprise everyone by making pancakes.

After stirring in a bit more mix to get the consistency right, he ladled two large circles into the pan, the batter setting with a sizzle. He waited, watching for bubbles to appear. Then heard his mother's footsteps overhead, and followed the sound of her steps down the stairs, knowing she'd be glad to see he'd already made coffee.

"Mornin'. . . . You must be Toby."

The man stood in the kitchen doorway, his hair messed and sticking straight up in places, nothing on but a pair of jeans, unbuttoned at the waist.

"Smells good down here. Don't mean to intrude. Just need to use the pot. . . . I'm Rick." He scratched his arm. "Your mother said it'd be okay."

It wasn't the first time Toby had been surprised on a Sunday morning by some half-naked guy wanting to use the bathroom. The man raked a hand across his whiskered jaw. Toby's gaze landed on the broad, hairy chest, then dropped to the huge feet. The nail of one of the big toes was black. The bones in both feet moved as the man shifted his weight.

Toby looked over the man's shoulder to the bathroom. The door was open. Then it was shut, the man inside. He heard the man's stream hitting the water. Loud. The toilet flushing. Toby didn't even look when the door opened, keeping his eyes on the pancakes, which now had thick-set bubbles and were starting to burn.

"I'll just pour a couple cups of coffee and get out of your way," the man said.

Toby heard him take two cups off the mug tree and move to the coffee on the counter.

"You don't happen to get the Sunday paper, do you?"

"Should've brought your own, maybe," Toby said, still staring at the pancakes.

"You're right," the man said. Then he was out of the kitchen, bare feet padding up the stairs.

Grabbing the spatula, Toby flipped the pancakes. First one, then the other, letting each splatter the ceiling and fall where it might. He turned off the stove, rushed to his room, threw on some clothes, and left, hating his mother for always surprising him like this. He thought this guy being here might mean that Mr. Fitness was out. Which was some consolation. Mr. Fitness had been a royal pain in the butt. Maybe the worst of any of his mom's boyfriends. Still, it stunk. Stunk being surprised by some stranger who hadn't even bothered to button his jeans all the way. Some guy with big feet and a hairy chest.

What was his name?

Toby was on his bike, racing for the school playground, the sun hurting his eyes.

Who gives a rat's ass!

SIX

By the middle of the next week, Leo had decided he was in love with Luanne. "It's the real thing," he told Toby in recess detention. "I get hot flashes just looking at her. People in love get hot flashes, don't they?"

Toby didn't know. He hadn't been in love since his first year of third grade. He couldn't remember if he'd gotten hot flashes or not. All he knew for sure was that the girl had the bluest eyes he'd ever seen, and that she always shared her cookies with him. He was still miffed at Mr. Toggert for flunking him.

"You think Luanne would go for me?" Leo said.

"Leo, please move to another table," Mrs. Ellison said. "You're supposed to be getting your work completed."

Leo made a face and moved. Toby flipped open his math book. He'd been in recess detention for three days straight for not finishing his work. Mr. Fenning had warned that if things didn't improve, Toby's mother would be called in for an early conference.

Pencil in hand, Toby stared out the long line of windows. Outside, kids from every grade were running and screaming. On the intermediate field, the fifth-and sixth-grade boys had a football game going. A group of sixth-grade girls stood nearby, some doing cartwheels. Between cartwheels, the girls watched the boys play.

Toby silently cursed Mr. Fenning for keeping him in. He pictured himself out there with the others, crashing past would-be tacklers and scoring touchdowns. Suddenly he saw Jeremy take a handoff from Jake. Toby about squirmed out of his seat as he followed the run, secretly urging the fifth graders to stop Jeremy.

The next thing Toby knew, Jeremy had run through a whole pack of guys. Hands went up, signifying *touchdown*. Jeremy raised the football high over his head, then spiked it hard to the ground. Toby watched as Jake and Brian and Michael all went up and patted Jeremy on the back. What ticked Toby off the most was the way some of the girls jumped up and down, like they were cheerleaders or something. Toby couldn't understand it. Most of the girls hated football.

When the bell rang, Toby rushed out of detention and hurried down the hall. Jeremy was flicking the ball up and down in one hand as he made for the classroom. Toby stepped into his path.

"You know I could take you in a fight, right?"

Jeremy turned red. "Maybe," he said, his jaw setting hard.

Toby took a step closer. Jeremy, only slightly shorter, didn't back up. Toby noticed how Jeremy's hair had grown out since the first day, how the scalp no longer showed through. Each boy took a breath and held it, their chests expanding and nearly touching, as a few stragglers gathered to see what would happen.

"Inside, everyone," Mr. Fenning's deep voice boomed suddenly. He had a coffee cup in hand, and gestured for Toby and Jeremy to move out of the flow of traffic. "What gives?" he said.

"Nothing," said Toby.

"Nothing," said Jeremy.

"Good," said Mr. Fenning. "Because if you two start anything, I'll be the one doing the finishing. Along with Mrs. Hawkins and your parents. Understood?"

Jeremy nodded first, then Toby. Mr. Fenning swung a hand toward the classroom. Toby walked in and slammed his book on his desk. He felt all bound up inside. All during reading class he felt like he might explode. He had his textbook opened to the story they were discussing, but he couldn't concentrate. It was like everything was a blur. How could a guy pay attention to some stupid story in a book when there were so many real-life things to think about? Like Jeremy scoring a touchdown. Like his mother and that guy with the black toe. Toby found himself thinking about that even when he didn't want to. How his mother had screamed that Toby was a good-for-nothing punk when he'd returned home from the playground on Sunday.

"You're a kid. I'm your mother. And I won't put up with this kind of crap again," she'd said, pointing to the dried bits of pancake on the ceiling. "I've got a life of my own. Grow up or you'll be out of here, I swear it!"

The story in the reading book was about some diver in Hawaii. Mr. Fenning asked if anyone had ever been to Hawaii.

"We might go during spring break," Veronica said.

"My sister has a grass skirt from there," Melissa said. "She got it on her honeymoon."

"Big deal," someone said.

"Well, it was!" Melissa shot back. "It was their honeymoon, and they sailed around on a boat."

Toby penciled a drawing of a palm tree on his desk, using the picture in the book as a guide. The newsflash blinked on all at once in his mind, like Christmas lights.

Mr. Blaine Kellogg, of cereal fame, today admitted under oath that his only son, Tobias Michael Scudder, of Vancouver, WA, is the one person in the entire world he really cares about. The multimillionaire went on to tell a jammed courtroom that he was just a young fool when he left Tobias some ten years ago, and that he

would make up for his mistake by taking Tobias on a
tour of the Hawaiian islands by sailboat. The boat will
be crewed by girls wearing grass skirts and bikini tops
made from coconut shells.

After reading, Mr. Fenning asked about how the
life-story books were going. Veronica said she'd already filled six pages. Leo asked if they could put
photos in the books, and Mr. Fenning said that would
be fine.

" 'Cause I've got one of me as a baby," Leo said.
"Naked!"

"It's *your* book," Mr. Fenning said. "You *have*
taken it home and started working on it, right?"

"Well, not really," Leo said. "I mean, I keep forgetting."

"Anyone else out there who has forgotten?" Mr.
Fenning asked.

Toby looked around. He saw two reluctant hands
move up. Mr. Fenning caught Toby's gaze, and Toby
looked away.

"The hardest part is just getting yourself started,"
Mr. Fenning said. "I guarantee that once you get a
couple of sentences down, the rest will be easy."

Toby was hardly listening. He'd already decided
to take an F on the assignment. But his ears perked up
when Mr. Fenning mentioned what they'd be doing in
science come Monday.

"You mean real eyes? Like real! And not plastic?"
Toby heard himself saying.

"The real McCoy. Dissecting cows' eyes will allow

us to learn both the structure of the eye and how it works."

"Neat!" several people said.

"Yuck!" several others added.

"What about the poor cows?"

"The eyes are purchased by the school from a slaughterhouse. Cows, as you know, are killed for their meat. I assume most of you eat hamburgers. Rather than throw out the eyes, slaughterhouses offer them to schools for educational purposes."

"Mr. Fenning, I won't be here," Josie said. "I can't."

"I can't!" Toby mimicked. Facing Josie, he used his fingers to pull back the skin above and below his eyes, so that they'd show their biggest. He had them opened so wide he could feel the air brushing cool against them. "I can't!" he said again.

"Toby, please," Mr. Fenning said. To Josie, he said, "Why don't you come to school and see how things go? If you find it really is too much for you, you can spend the period in the library."

There was a loud chorus of *phew*s from the girls.

Toby turned to Leo, who gave an "all right!" shake of his fist. Toby smiled, returning the salute. It was like a wind had suddenly blown over him, prying loose his bound-up feeling and sweeping it out the window. *We're gonna cut up a cow's eye,* he thought. *We're gonna do some science!*

□   □   □

Leo was in a state of bliss at lunch on Monday. Mr. Fenning had given everyone a lab partner for the cow's-eye experiment. Leo's partner was Luanne.

"And she's even wearing her coyote shirt," he said. "Like she knew I liked it special or something."

Toby doubted that was the case, since neither Luanne nor anyone else had had any idea who their partner would be before they'd come to school that morning. As for Toby, he'd crossed both his fingers and toes when Mr. Fenning had started announcing partners from his list. It was clear right away that the partners would be boy-girl. Toby hoped for Josie. He gave Denny Sasser's seat in front of him a mighty kick, then broke two pencils in half, when Mr. Fenning said, "Toby and Veronica."

Still, even having Veronica as a partner wasn't enough to dampen Toby's anticipation. He kept things well focused at lunch.

"I feel like I could eat a cow today," he said.

"Me too," said Leo.

"Hey," Toby said, "this soup looks like it's got eyeballs floating around in it!" He stabbed a floating potato piece with his fork and held it up. "Yep, thought so.

"Mmmmmm," he added, popping the piece in his mouth.

"I hope you're going to act like a normal human being," Veronica said when the desks and partners had been paired for the experiment. She kept looking from the board to her paper, copying the diagram of the eye that Mr. Fenning had instructed everyone to draw and label.

"I'll act the way I want," Toby said, rushing through his own drawing. He was sorry his wish hadn't come true. He'd hoped that Veronica might come down with some horrible disease before science and have to go home.

Mr. Fenning and some kids were passing out equipment for the big event. Toby looked back to see Leo and Luanne sitting side by side. He thought the size difference between the two made them look a little like Sylvester and Tweety Bird. When Toby caught Leo's eye, Leo made sure Luanne wasn't looking, then stiffly pushed out his lips as if to whistle or kiss, his eyes widening in a *hubba-hubba* look.

"Newspaper, paper plate, razor blade, tweezers, and paper towels," Mr. Fenning said. "Looks like everyone's set."

He opened the front cupboard, lifted two huge glass jars from the shelf, and brought them to the table positioned in front of the class. Floating around in some kind of clear liquid preservative were dark eyeballs shrouded in masses of gray-white tissue.

"They look like oysters!" someone said.

"They're gross!"

"Now, now," Mr. Fenning said. "You're all big sixth graders, remember?" Using a slotted spoon, he began passing out the eyes.

"It doesn't look like an oyster at all," Veronica

said when the eye had been placed on her and Toby's plate.

Toby sniffed at the smell. "It looks more like something for Halloween," he said, picking up the eye and raising it to his forehead. He pulled his lower lip under his top teeth, hoping the teeth looked like fangs.

"Mr. *Fenning!*" Veronica screeched.

Toby held up the eye long enough for others to notice. The reaction was a combination of laughter and shudders.

"You've just used up your one and only warning, Mr. Scudder," Mr. Fenning said. "One more mistake and you're out."

"Stop poking it," Josie called out to her partner, Brian.

"Perhaps we should just cancel the whole thing," Mr. Fenning said.

"No!" most everyone said.

"Then quit the goofing and listen up.

"The eyeball is situated in a cushion of muscle and fat," he announced when all was quiet. "Take your razor and carefully cut away the fatty tissue."

Toby grabbed the razor. Veronica took the tweezers to steady the spongy eye for Toby to cut. Toby was surprised at the amount of pressure it took before the first slice fell away, his nostrils flaring from the sharp, chemical smell of the preservative.

"The cornea is the tough, clear covering on the top of the eyeball," continued Mr. Fenning. "Slice through this covering. The aqueous humor, a thin liquid that cushions the lens below, will probably seep out as you cut through."

"Let me," Veronica said. "You already had a chance to cut."

Toby reluctantly gave up the razor.

"This cornea thing is made of iron," someone said.

"Press harder," Mr. Fenning said.

Veronica pressed harder. Others must have been pressing harder too, because suddenly the room was filled with splatting sounds, followed by cries of "You got it on me!" and "I can't stand it!"

Toby couldn't remember school ever being so much fun. He took his pencil to the sharpener in order to more fully enjoy the event. Jeremy and Melissa were nearest to the sharpener, and they had already sliced through their cornea. A pool of the liquid humor stuff lay on their plate, slowly spreading to encircle the pieces of cut-off muscle tissue. The eye itself, in the center of the plate, had been whittled to the size of a giant gumball.

"I think I want to be a scientist," Toby heard Jeremy tell Melissa. "Dissecting doesn't bother me at all."

Melissa had the glazed look of one of those girls you see in beer commercials. Toby recalled how Melissa was one of the cheerleaders he'd seen jumping up and down after Jeremy's touchdown that time. Jeremy kept smiling. Toby sharpened harder.

"Jeremy said he's done this before," Melissa told Toby as though it mattered. "In his other school."

"Big deal," Toby said. He stopped cranking. "See if he's done this before." And before he had a chance to really think about it, Toby swept his hand across their plate, grabbing up the eye.

"Hey!" Melissa said.

"Do *what?*" Jeremy said.

"THIS!" Toby said. In a single, lightning-quick motion, he opened his mouth, popped the eye inside, and swallowed hard. Swallowed twice. "Ahhh," he said, his throat closing over its prey. "Less filling, tastes great."

"HE ATE IT!" someone screamed. "HE ATE IT!"

"Toby ate a cow's eye! I saw it!"

"OUT!" Mr. Fenning ordered. "In the hall . . . now!"

Toby strutted across the front of room toward the door. He could have been on some float at a parade, everyone looking up at him. The faces out there in the crowd showed shock and disgust. But something else, too. Awe, maybe. Even more than that. Reverence. Reverence at knowing that none of them would have the guts to do such a thing.

Respect, Toby thought. And smiling from his parade float, he waved.

It was only when he had reached the hall, closing the door behind him, that Toby realized something wasn't right. The chemical smell from the eye seemed to flush through his whole body. With a gasp, he realized that the eye hadn't gone all the way down—it was still there, partway down his throat, stuck. Toby opened and closed his mouth, his tongue feeling thick and clingy. Thick and clingy with slime. Some of that fatty stuff from the eye had coated the inside of his mouth. He could taste it, too! The preservative sharp as turpentine. The ball in his throat came up, then moved down to its stuck position. The smell was overpowering. He tried swallowing again, the slime spreading like rancid butter over his tongue to the back of his throat. The ball was on the move again.

Dizzy and retching, hand clamped to his mouth, Toby ran.

SEVEN

"Toby? . . . Toby, you in there?"

The door of the stall hung partly open behind him. Although only a few minutes had passed, Toby thought he'd been kneeling over the bowl with one hand on the handle for hours. He spit again, then flushed for the third time. It seemed to take all his strength to push himself back from the rim.

Mr. Fenning held the door open. "You get sick?"

Still on his knees, Toby nodded.

"Maybe it wasn't such a smart thing to do," the teacher said.

Toby brushed away a thread of saliva he could see dangling past his chin. "Please don't tell. They'll all laugh."

Mr. Fenning blew out a sigh. "I see your problem," he said. "If I go back to class and say the mighty Toby was on the floor in the bathroom puking his guts out, it might be pretty embarrassing, right?"

Not embarrassing, Toby thought. *The ultimate worst thing that could possibly happen.*

"Maybe I can make you a deal," the teacher went on.

"You mean you won't tell?"

"I didn't say that. What I said was that perhaps we can forge a deal."

"What kind of a deal?" Toby said, hope powering him to his feet.

Mr. Fenning backed out into the wide, tiled walkway beyond the stalls. Still wobbly, Toby joined him.

"Let me think on that," the teacher said. "Right now, what you need to do is to go back to class and apologize to everyone for causing such a ruckus. And not a peep out of you for the rest of the afternoon. Stay in your seat after dismissal. We'll talk."

Toby walked out, Mr. Fenning's hard leather heels echoing behind him.

□   □   □

MY LIFE
by TOBY SCUDDER

Toby stared at the book. He lay on the unmade bed, elbows propped, chin cupped in his palms. His legs swung up and down, his sneakers smacking the foot of the mattress and rebounding. Smacking and rebounding. He thought things had turned out pretty well, considering. When he'd returned to class after getting sick, he'd found he was something of a hero.

"You really did it, didn't you?" Jake whispered as Toby marched back to his seat. "You swallowed it!"

Even the girls seemed impressed. Toby overheard Sarah Nishida tell Gina Girardi that it was the funniest, creepiest thing she had ever seen. And when the dissection was over, and people returned to their original seats, Josie said, "You're crazy, Toby, you know that?"

"Everybody went nuts after you left," Leo said when Toby came out to the playground after his meeting with Mr. Fenning. "You're a legend, man. What'd Fenning say?"

"Just another warning," Toby said.

It wasn't quite that. Toby and Mr. Fenning had made a deal. No one would ever know about the incident at the toilet bowl. All Toby had to do was agree to write in his life-story book. "Ten pages at the very least," Mr. Fenning had said. "Ten pages and my lips are sealed forever. But if, when the books are due, I find you've written anything less, then, in accordance with the deal, I get to tell the class about an interesting incident that occurred that day of the cow's eye dissection." They'd shaken hands on it.

Now, staring at the book, Toby wondered how he'd ever be able to do that much writing. He couldn't think of a single thing worth putting down. His life was your typical, boring twelve-year-old life. There wasn't much to say. Not much had happened to him. He hadn't won any prizes. Done anything great. His grades were always the worst. He could play a hard game of football, and had dreams of becoming a professional wrestler. But so what? A lot of people could play football and dreamed of being athletes. He'd been born in Phoenix, moved to Vancouver, and here he was still. Who would be interested in a life like that? Even Mr. Fenning, who was probably used to reading boring student papers, would fall dead asleep reading such junk.

Toby looked up to see Slammer and Crusher eyeing him from their bowl, their tails slowly swishing as they bobbed in place. With a sigh, he turned open the book's thick cover. The blank page that looked back at him was divided by lines, lines he would have to fill. How many lines were there? He counted them. Twenty-five. Twenty-five times ten. *No*, he suddenly remembered. Mr. Fenning had said both sides equaled one page. That would make twenty-five times twenty! Leo was right. The guy *was* a slave-driver!

Feeling a sudden pang of hunger, Toby rolled off the bed. He checked the clock in the kitchen, then poured himself a bowl of Frosted Flakes, adding two spoons of sugar and enough milk to make the flakes float. Carrying the bowl to the front room, he grabbed the remote. What popped on was this show about bounty hunting in Alaska. There was this guy named Zack who captured live animals for zoos. In the past, the lady announcer said, bounty hunters would get money just to kill the animals, but now you could be a bounty hunter, make money, and keep the animals alive.

Toby put a heaping spoonful of flakes in his mouth. He liked the idea of living out in the wilds where no one would be there to boss you around. He also liked the fact that Zack wore a thick sheepskin-lined parka.

The lady doing the interview seemed to think that Zack was the best thing to come along since Guess? jeans. "You built this wonderful log cabin all by yourself?" she said, like she didn't already know the answer.

"Yes, ma'am," Zack said. "It's got all the comforts of home. I may be a loner, but I like life's little pleasures."

Toby was especially impressed by Zack's outdoor Jacuzzi, and by the satellite dish that Zack said kept him in touch with the outside world.

When the show was over, Toby got ready for bed. He pounded the floor of his room twice to tell Gordon to lower the volume of his boom box down below. Gordon's answer of "Stuff it!" cut sharply through the boards.

The book still lay on the bed, and Toby tossed it to the floor. He said good night to Slammer and Crusher. Then he turned off the light and slipped under the covers, the darkness amplifying the grunts and screeches of whatever tape Gordon was playing.

Replaying the day's events in his mind, Toby's thoughts took a sudden turn. He pictured Mr. Fenning telling the whole class how Toby had puked up the eye. "What a fake!" he heard Sarah tell Gina. "I never believed he swallowed it in the *first* place," Veronica would say.

Toby rolled to the edge of the bed and reached for the lamp, the light cutting into his eyes. He snatched the book from the floor, then fumbled for the pencil that had poked his back when he'd first gotten into bed.

This is Toby Scudder. Forced to write in this stupid book. But it doesn't have to be neat. It can be as SLOPPY as I want. I hate writing, see? So if I have to do this, I'm gonna do it my way. First thing, I was born. Whoop-whoop! Mom says I was a big baby. I'm still big. My father's name is Blaine Kellogg. He's long gone. Sometimes I think about him. I might get a newsflash or something. Like tonight when I was watching this show: *Mr. Blaine Kellogg, bounty hunter, after capturing a grizzly bear, admitted that though he was pleased with his outdoor Jacuzzi and satellite dish, it was all nothing compared to the joy he felt when his son Tobias Michael Scudder was born some twelve years ago.*

It was a strange feeling that came over Toby. He'd just about filled one whole page—well, one side of a page—and it hadn't killed him. He flipped the cover closed and set the book on the nightstand beside

Slammer and Crusher, who floated, as if sleeping, inside the doughnut hole of their rock.

After killing the light, Toby moved to the center of the bed. He yanked the blanket up to his ears the way he liked it, and had nearly dozed off when he heard the car pull up in the drive. The car door slamming. Twice. Then voices, outside on the porch. The key clicking in the lock. The door refusing to open cleanly. A kick. And the familiar pop of release.

"Shhh."

A laugh. A giggle. Whispers.

"Ouch! Turn on the damn light."

"Shhh!"

"Are they asleep?"

"Of course they're asleep. It's past midnight."

"Toby?"

The door cracked open. Toby didn't answer, his eyes pressed shut.

When the whispers and footsteps moved to the kitchen, Toby turned over hard in the dark. He grabbed the pillow, punching a new, deeper hole for his head. And kept right on punching . . . five, six, seven, eight times, as if trying to drill the pillow straight through the mattress. With a groan he flipped the pillow over his head and held the ends tight against his ears, a humming silence replacing the sounds coming from the kitchen.

Mr. Fitness was back.

EIGHT

Leo had his life-story book with him the next day. He wanted to show Luanne his baby picture. "Just in case she likes me," he told Toby on the way to school.

Toby chuckled when he saw the picture taped to the first page. There was Leo, lying on some kind of rug thing, without a stitch on. The rug thing was green, surrounded by blue material. The background showed a painting of a pond with lily pads all over.

"It's like I'm sitting on a lily pad in a pond," Leo said. "Get it?"

Toby nodded. He thought Leo was pretty brave to be taking the picture to school. He knew he'd be embarrassed for anyone to see a picture of him without any clothes, baby or not.

"I've got it all thought out," Leo said. "My mom and my sisters go nuts over babies, saying how cute they are. All women think babies are cute, even when the babies drool or poop. They talk goofy to them and say how adorable they are."

"So?" Toby said.

"So, Luanne is a girl. She'll think I'm cute, too."

Toby wasn't quite sure he understood. But he was already looking forward to being there when Leo showed the picture to Luanne.

When they got to school, they found Josie and Melissa and some other girls standing outside the classroom, girl-talking. Luanne was there too, but off to the side, studying the new artwork that Mr. Myers, the art teacher, had put up on the wall.

"Where's Mr. Fenning?" Leo said.

Toby ducked his head into the classroom. "It's okay. He's in the back, messing with the bulletin board."

Jake came out of the room when he saw Toby. "Hey," he said.

Veronica came striding toward them with her violin case in hand. Her mouth flew open at the sight of Leo's book. "You're not supposed to bring in those until they're due," she said. "Don't ya know?"

"No," Leo said. "I don't know anything. I was hit by a bus on the way to school and I've forgotten every stupid rule this school has."

Toby laughed. Veronica huffed her way into the classroom, appearing again an instant later without her violin case.

Josie had come over at Veronica's mention of Leo's

book. "How much have you written?" Josie asked. "I've got four pages done."

"Not much," Leo said. He saw Luanne finish with the artwork and drift toward the group. "But it's the picture I wanted you all to see." He looked at Toby.

Toby smiled. "They're too young," he said.

"What?" Josie said, bug-eyed.

"You got a girlie picture in there?" Jake said. "Let's see."

"If it is, I'm telling," Veronica said.

"Who's got a dirty picture?" Melissa said. "You're lying."

Leo shrugged as if he wouldn't be responsible for anything past this point, then opened his book and held it out for everyone to see. There was just the tiniest fraction of a moment of silence while everyone looked. Then laughter. Or mostly laughter.

"Oh, is *that* all," Veronica said with a wave of her hand. "I've got *lots* of those."

"Nice buns, Leo," Josie said with a giggle.

"You were a little shrimp even then," Melissa said.

"Not a shrimp," Leo said. "Can't you see? I was a *frog!* Don't you know lily pads when you see them? I'm cute, aren't I?" His gaze rose up from the book to find Luanne.

"All babies are cute," Melissa said, looking at the picture again. "Even Leo!"

Toby couldn't tell if Luanne's blush was due to her laughter or to Leo's dreamy-eyed stare. Then the bell rang, and it was over.

"I knew the picture would be a breakthrough," Leo said as he and Toby followed the others inside. "Luanne came right over to us. She laughed, too. And it wasn't a mean laugh, either. I don't think I ever heard her laugh before."

The fact that everyone else had laughed didn't seem to matter to Leo. Toby figured that's what people meant when they said that love was blind. "You got it bad," he said.

"I know," Leo said, before splitting off to his seat. "I don't know what I'll do if I move."

"Huh?" Toby said.

"Seats, everyone," Mr. Fenning said. "Let's hit it!"

Leo shook his head at Toby, like it wasn't a good idea to keep talking.

"Seat, Toby," Mr. Fenning said. "Let's get started."

Toby wondered if he'd heard right. What Leo said. He turned in his chair to give Leo a *what gives?* look. Leo was too busy poking around in his desk to look up.

After the opening business of attendance and lunch count was finished, Mr. Fenning dropped a new project on the class. "On Friday we'll be going down to Ms. Lorimer's first-grade class to meet our Kiddie Pals."

"Our what?" several people said.

"Well, I haven't quite come up with a term I'm happy with. But what it amounts to is that each of you will be given a first grader as a pal. Each week we'll go down to Ms. Lorimer's room and do something together. You'll work with your pal. Read together. Play games. Draw. Write stories . . . that kind of thing.

"We're going to start this Friday with sharing books. So have a book ready to share with your pal. The first graders have already been told, and they're ecstatic to know that they'll be working with a real, live, honest-to-goodness sixth grader! Several parents have already called Ms. Lorimer to say that all their little Johnnie or Susie can talk about is how they're going to have a sixth-grade pal for the year."

Several people thought it was a good idea. Others were less enthusiastic.

"As long as I don't get my brother," Jeremy said.

"If his brother's anything like him," Toby whispered to Denny, "the kid must be a wuss in the making."

"I pity whoever gets my sister," Gina said. "She's into toilet words. And making herself burp. It's disgusting."

"Let's try looking on the bright side," Mr. Fenning said.

To Toby the whole thing sounded like more work.

□   □   □

Toby had to stay in to finish his social studies workbook pages during morning recess. He slopped it finished, for once not caring about what Jeremy or the others were doing on the playground. He was a lot more concerned with what Leo had said about moving.

"You can't move," he finally blurted to Leo at lunch. "I mean, we're buddies, right?"

"Yeah," Leo said. "Sure. Mom's just talking about it, that's all. She's mad at me as usual. She said a boy should be with a man during the teen years. She said she doesn't think she could stand it. She says she doesn't want any more gray hairs. She's afraid I'm gonna turn into a teen sex fiend or a serial killer or something."

"You sounded like it might really happen," Toby said. "That you might really move."

"That's just the way it came out," Leo said. "And besides, my dad would have to say yes, and I think he's changed his mind again, especially since he got moved back to graveyard shift at the plant."

"Well, it'd be dumb for a guy to move during sixth grade," Toby said. "Real dumb. Maybe you shouldn't do anything stupid to make your mom mad—if you don't want to move, I mean. You don't, do you?"

"Heck no," Leo said. "This is our year to be at the top of the heap. I wouldn't want to blow that."

Toby let out a yell, a cowboy yell, that caused Mrs. Zimmerman, the staff assistant, to come running over. "That's enough," she said.

"I couldn't help it," Toby said. "I had a sudden vision I was in an old-time cowboy movie—get along, little dogies," he added, snapping his wrist as if lashing a whip. Leo laughed. Mrs. Zimmerman folded her arms over her chest, but she didn't seem all that mad.

"You can't blame 'im," Leo said, lifting the bun off his burger. "It's these cow patties we got today."

"Yeah," Toby said. "If I had a chain saw, I might even be able to eat mine."

□   □   □

Andrea popped in that night do her laundry.

Toby put two frozen dinners in the microwave that sometimes worked and sometimes didn't. This time it did. "You want the steak or the chicken?" he asked when the dinners were done. He lifted the plastic covering from each.

"They both look gross," Andrea said. "I'll take the chicken."

They ate in the front room on tray tables, watching *Wheel of Fortune*. During commercials Toby asked Andrea about hair college and Andrea asked Toby about school.

"I can't believe old Hawk-Eye Hawkins is still there," Andrea said. "She giving you any trouble?"

"She's a pain where the sun don't shine," Toby said.

"What about your teacher?"

"He thinks we're in college or something," Toby said. "It's like he doesn't even know it's our last year at Broughton. Whoever heard of sixth graders working?" He finished up his peaches, then said, "You know that guy's back. Mom's going out with him again."

"Which one?"

"Doug. Mr. Fitness. The one who thinks he's Arnold Schwarzenegger."

"The hunk?" Andrea said.

"You like him?"

"Not particularly. But he got Mom through her turning-forty trauma. She says he makes her feel young again."

"He bosses her around," Toby said.

"Hey, she puts up with it, what can we do? If he's as much of a jerk as you say, she'll see it sooner or later. . . . Want my pears?"

Toby shook his head.

When Andrea left, Toby called Leo and asked if he could come over. "We can call up girls or something. Then watch TV."

"I can't," Leo said. "I have to do the dishes. And Mom's having a migraine over my room."

After a couple of hours of TV, during which he polished off what was left of a carton of marble fudge ice cream, Toby was bored enough to go to his room and pick up his life-story book. "Maybe I can squeeze out another page," he told Slammer and Crusher, who didn't appear all that interested.

Write, write, write. Stupid, stupid, stupid. Boring, boring, boring. I was born, I said that. What else? My mom and dad were never married. BIG DEAL!

Mom said she'd had enough of marriage with Carl Scudder—that's where my last name comes in. Mom kept the Scudder name even after her and Carl got divorced. That's why I'm a Scudder too. Maybe if my real dad ever comes back to claim me, I can be a Kellogg like him. I wouldn't mind having a last name that's different from that scuzz ball, Gordon. Besides being my half-brother, Gordon also has only half a brain.

Here's a picture of Gordon's brain.

Gordon wants to go into the Marine Corps after high school. That's if he ever passes. I told him the Marines are looking for a few good men with whole brains. So that leaves him out.

Mom says Blaine Kellogg left when I was two. I don't remember. There are exactly six pictures of Blaine and me when I was a baby. In all of them he's holding me, and looking surprised. I'm smiling in two pictures, probably because I've got this cool doggie-biscuit-shaped rattle in my hand and

I'm waving it (I can tell I'm waving it because it's blurred). Sometimes I wonder if maybe I hit my father in the head with the rattle. And that's why he looks so surprised.

I'm sitting on my father's lap in the other four pictures too, but I don't have the rattle. Instead of smiling, I'm making weird faces, like I just filled my pants and I know it'll be a while before the smell gets bad enough so someone will change me. I'm pretty sure my father knows what I've done. That must be why he's surprised in these pictures too.

But this is what I don't get. If my father could put up with me through all that messy baby stuff (Mom says I cried a lot and my father got up and walked me around the patio where we were living in Phoenix), then why did he leave just when I was over all that? Cause Mom says I was toilet trained by two, which she thinks is a record. And that once I stopped teething, I always slept right through the night. I just think it's weird that my father would leave then, when the hard part was over.

Toby stopped, his hand aching from so much writing. Slammer and Crusher were chasing each other around their bowl. Toby wondered if fish ever got dizzy. He knew people did. *All that writing*, he thought.

NINE

"Quiet," Mr. Fenning kept saying. "Single file."

No one seemed to be paying any attention. The class tramped down the long hall to the primary-grade wing, chatting and carrying books for sharing with their soon-to-be-announced Kiddie Pals.

When their noise passed the office, Mrs. Hawkins rushed out, hawk eyes peeled. She put a finger to her mouth and looked at Mr. Fenning, as if to ask if this was the best he could do at controlling his class.

Toby and Leo were discussing tomorrow night's *Main Event,* in which El Gigante was to meet Steve Austin. Toby stopped talking when he saw Mrs. Hawkins. If anyone would be picked out for talking, he knew it would be him, and he sure didn't want to have to sit in the office when everyone else was having a good time messing around in Ms. Lorimer's room.

The day before, during library time, Toby had chosen a book he'd remembered from when he was younger. A book that one of his teachers had read to the class. He couldn't remember what grade he'd been in or who the teacher was. But he remembered the book because it was a funny story about a snake and was written by some guy whose last name was Kellogg. Toby had gone to the K section of the picture books and found the book right away. He was surprised to find his name printed in pencil on the card in the back of the book. The letters were big, taking up two spaces, and were all uneven, the O flat on top and the tail of the Y swerving sharply to the left as if someone had knocked his arm when he was writing. The card was old and yellowed and no longer used now that checkouts were done by computer.

Leo had chosen a book on sharks, mostly because there was a picture in it showing a person whose arm had been chomped off in an attack. "In California, they closed the beach to swimming one day because of a shark sighting," he had told Toby for the hundredth time. "My uncle had his binoculars, and we tried to see it. Then I gave up looking for the shark and used the binoculars to check out the babes instead."

The first-grade classroom was hot and airless. Mr. Fenning had everyone line up single file along the walls. Toby really liked how the little kids were instantly quiet when they came in. It was like they were holding their breath. Like they were thinking, *Look, sixth graders!*

Ms. Lorimer welcomed everyone. "We've been looking forward to your visit," she said. "Haven't we, class?"

The little kids squirmed in their seats, nodding and looking like this would be one of the biggest events in their lives. One boy, a miniature version of Jeremy—short hair and all—kept pointing to where Jeremy stood in line. "That's my brother!" the kid finally blurted when Ms. Lorimer paused.

"See," a girl said, pointing to Gina. "That one right there . . . she's my sister!"

Everyone looked at Jeremy and Gina, whose faces flushed red.

"When you get your pal," Ms. Lorimer said, "just find a space where you can talk quietly and get to know each other. I see you sixth graders have books to share. My kids have also chosen a book or story to share."

As Ms. Lorimer read each name from her class list, Mr. Fenning named a sixth grader. He just went around, beginning with Brian Loper, who was the first person in line along the back wall. It was clear that neither Mr. Fenning nor Ms. Lorimer was concerned about whether you got a pal of your own sex. In fact it worked out that most of the pairs were boy-girl, which accounted for quite a few groans, especially from those sixth-grade boys who'd been hoping for a boy.

"Yeah!" Leo said when it was his turn and he ended up with some kid named Simon. Toby was next, and there were only about six or seven little kids left.

"Megan McDaniels," Ms. Lorimer said. A girl wearing a pair of faded brown overalls leaped up. Toby had noticed the girl more than once during the pairings. She'd been just about jumping out of her seat with excitement the whole time.

"Ready for your pal, Megan?" Mr. Fenning said with a laugh.

The little girl nodded, so hard her carrot-colored pigtails bounced up and down.

"Looks like Toby's up next," Mr. Fenning said. "Megan McDaniels, meet Toby Scudder."

Toby couldn't hide his disappointment at getting a girl. Mr. Fenning gave him a look that said, *Now, don't be cruel.* With a sigh, Toby went to Megan's desk as the last few pairings were made.

"Where should we go?" Toby said.

Megan's huge eyes swept the room. She looked as if she'd been told to pick out anything she wanted at Toys "R" Us. "There!" she said. And she led Toby to an unoccupied place in the back near a metal rack of books.

By this time the room was alive with chatter. Toby sat down against the wall below a kitten poster.

"Want a pillow?" Megan said.

Toby shrugged.

Megan ran to a box labeled "Soft and Cuddly" beside Ms. Lorimer's desk and fished out a blue pillow.

"I don't need it," Toby said when she came back. "Aw, maybe I will," he added when he saw her smile droop.

Megan squiggled down beside him, both their backs against the wall. "See?" she said proudly. "This is my reader. I've been practicing. Want to hear?"

Again Toby shrugged, his gaze moving around to see what was happening. For the most part everyone was sharing, some more reluctantly than others. Mr. Fenning and Ms. Lorimer were both circulating, stopping here and there to help out or to threaten those who were having a tough time getting started.

Toby was surprised at what a good reader Megan was. She read a story about a kid who's going to stay overnight at his friend's house. The kid's worried that his friend will laugh at him for taking his teddy bear along. In the end the friend pulls out a teddy bear of his own. And the two boys are each relieved that the other needs a bear to fall asleep too.

"Now it's your turn," Megan said.

Toby put his book on his lap. "It's about a snake," he said.

Megan's eyes lit up.

"A big, fat boa constrictor," Toby said, pointing to the cover. "Who likes to eat laundry."

Megan giggled, rubbing her hands together. Toby thought they were the smallest hands he'd ever seen.

He read slow, not wanting to mess up in front of a first grader. Megan giggled the whole way through.

She kept pointing out things in the pictures that Toby hadn't noticed. "Look!" she'd say. "Oh, look!"

"That was the best story I ever heard in my whole life," she said when Toby had finished.

"You liked it?"

"Mmmm-hmmm! Someday I'll be able to read as good as you."

Toby accepted the praise. "You're a good reader already," he said.

"My mom and I read every night," she said. "My dad, too, when he's not working. I think stories are the best. Don't you like stories?"

"Yeah," Toby said. "They're all right."

Suddenly the lights went off, then came on again. "I'm afraid our time is up," Ms. Lorimer said. "First graders, please thank your new pal and return to your seat."

"Sixth graders, line up at the front," Mr. Fenning said.

"Thank you for being my pal," Megan said, pigtails bobbing.

"Sure," Toby said.

"We'll see you all next week," Ms. Lorimer said.

Toby squeezed into line beside Leo. Then the line was moving out the door. Several of the first graders were waving to their pals. Megan did more than wave. Jumping out of her seat, she ran up to Toby just as he reached the door. "Here," she said, shoving something into his hand.

"Looks like you're famous," Leo said. "My kid spent twenty minutes reading two pages. I had to tell him almost every word. What'd she give you?"

Toby opened his hand. What he saw was a piece of dirty pink eraser, the ends nibbled and lined with tooth marks.

Leo laughed. Toby did too. His first thought was to fling the eraser at Josie or Brian or somebody else farther up in line. But he didn't. He stuffed it in his pocket instead.

□   □   □

They had P.E. later in the day, outside. Mr. Fenning demonstrated how to punt a football. He slipped once in midair, landing on his bottom to thunderous applause. Then people picked partners and took turns on their own. Toby and Leo worked together at the far end of the field. Toby could punt a mile. His went the farthest of anybody's. "You got a foot of steel there, Toby," Mr. Fenning called from where he stood near the backstop.

"Hey, what about *my* foot?" Leo said. Holding the ball in both his hands, he took two quick steps and let go. His foot caught the ball and sent it straight up, directly over his head. Both he and Toby laughed.

"Good height," Mr. Fenning said. "Your distance needs a little work."

Toby took another turn, his foot hitting the ball solidly, the ball sailing high and far. He felt good about Mr. Fenning's comment. *Tobias Michael Scud-*

der, he thought. *Foot of Steel.* Knowing he could kick better than Jeremy added to his good feeling. He'd checked out Jeremy's punts first thing. He knew Jeremy was faster and could throw more accurately than he could. But Toby's punts went farther and had a lot more hang time than Jeremy's.

Mr. Fenning had everyone run a lap around the field, then they went in. "How 'bout stopping down to see Ms. Blankenship?" Mr. Fenning told Toby at the classroom door.

"What for?" Toby said.

"She made a special request. Just wants to talk. She says you two are friends."

Toby made a face. Then he remembered math was coming up, and he decided seeing the counselor wasn't such a bad idea. He took his time in the hall, checking out the bulletin boards and display cases on the way.

Ms. Blankenship's office was off the gym. Entering it was like entering a submarine, it was that small. It had been converted from an old shower room, and Toby always thought he could still smell the damp and heat and sweat from when the school had been a high school. There was a tiny window, too high to see out of, with an old, rusted fan that didn't work.

The door was open. Toby knocked once and looked inside.

"Hi!" the counselor said. "Great you could make it!" She pointed to the chair in front of her desk, then cleared away some papers she'd been working on.

Toby sat, checking out the new posters on the walls. He thought the best was the one showing a picture of a diapered baby whose nose was crinkled. BABY PHILOSOPHY, the poster read. IF IT STINKS, CHANGE IT!

The phone rang and Ms. Blankenship frowned. "Sorry," she said before taking the call. Toby noticed that she'd cut her hair short over the summer. Her glasses were different, too—the new frames wide and colored blue. Toby remembered seeing the same sea blue in a film Mrs. Childs had shown the year before. The film had been about this place in Australia called the Great Barrier Reef. There were gobs of neon-colored fish swimming between layers of razor-sharp coral.

"It's such a beautiful place," Mrs. Childs had said. "And dangerous. Countless snorkelers have learned just how dangerous. One slip-up, one brush against the razor coral, and your skin is peeled off like masking tape." It was the only time Toby remembered paying attention the whole year.

"Guess what," Ms. Blankenship said brightly when she'd recradled the phone. "You're not in trouble. Just wanted to check in with you. See how things are going."

Toby figured what she said was only partly true. He was pretty sure Mr. Fenning had talked to her about how he was behind in all his subjects. Most likely Mrs. Hawkins had filled her in some, too. Toby had been sent to see Mrs. Hawkins three times the past two weeks. Twice for yelling things out in class. And once for tripping Brian Loper as Brian walked past him on his way to the drinking fountain. Brian had accused Toby of taking his Mississippi Riverboat pen, the one with the boat that moved up and down through a thick liquid whenever the pen was tipped. Toby had never even thought about taking the dumb pen.

"So how's school?"

"Fine."

"Good. And at home?"

"Okay."

"How's your mom?"

"Fine."

"I remember you saying something last year about some man she was dating. I can't remember his name. He still in the picture?"

"Mom and me and him went camping once over the summer. He hasn't been around much lately—I mean, he wasn't for a while. He's back, though . . . maybe."

"As I recall, you didn't much care for him. What's his name again?"

"Mr. Fitness. Doug, really. He's into his body."

She laughed. "I remember now. He's a muscle guy, huh?"

"He's a butthead," Toby said. "He makes fun of me 'cause I'm fat."

"Fat comes and goes," she said. "At least it's something you may be able to do something about if you want. It's the stuff a person can't do anything about that makes things tough."

Toby wished he could do something about Mr. Fitness.

"It's possible to get along with someone even if you don't like them," Ms. Blankenship said. "Keeping your distance is probably the best way. You can be a duck, too, and let the cruel or unfair stuff the person says or does just slide off your back."

Toby pictured himself with feathers and wings. He figured he'd waddle worse than all the other ducks. He shrugged. "Can I go now?" He knew he hadn't wasted enough of math period, but figured he could take his time getting back to class.

Ms. Blankenship tossed the pencil she'd been fingering onto the desk with a fake sigh. "You don't even feel sorry for me, do you? Here I am trying to make conversation so I don't have to go back to all this dreary paperwork. And you want to leave. You're cruel, Toby Scudder!"

Back in the hall, Toby ran into Mrs. Hawkins, who asked about the kind of day he was having.

"Super and excellent and awesome and every other great thing you could think of," he said.

"My," she said, kind of flustered.

He continued down the hall, his steps quickening, glad to be putting distance between himself and the principal. Once he'd turned the corner and saw that no one was about, he bent at the knees and waddled. Waddled right past the open doorway of Mrs. Childs' room, where he let out a "Quack!" for good measure. Then he straightened and ran hard.

□   □   □

NEWSFLASH: Learning that his son, Tobias Michael Scudder, "Foot of Steel," did not die of childhood measles, as previously thought, Mr. Blaine Kellogg today swore to locate his former family and to patch things up with Mrs. Sandra Scudder, his former almost-wife. Mr. Kellogg will then move the family—except for Gordon, who will be forced to stay in the cramped little dump of a house on Aspen Street until the other half of his brain grows in—to a private island off the coast of Australia . . . where Tobias will learn how to snorkel without cutting himself on coral while continuing his research on the mysteries of fish.

TEN

Toby hated anchovies. Even the smell made him sick to his stomach.

"We'll go halves," his mother said. "You can have pepperoni on your half."

It was Saturday night and they were sitting at a window table at Godfather's Pizza after going shopping. Toby wore his new Nikes. They weren't the expensive ones, but they were okay. And Toby needed them. His old ones were so worn, he hadn't even bothered to take them home. "Just toss 'em," he'd told the store clerk, who had picked up the shoes by the laces, holding them away from him like he expected poisonous spiders to come crawling out before he reached the wastebasket.

After ordering at the counter, Toby filled his glass at the pop machine. He took the long way back to the table, checking out his new shoes as he walked.

The pizza was good—hardly any spaces between the pepperoni slices. Toby would have enjoyed it even more if he hadn't had to smell the anchovies coming from his mother's side of the table.

"I wish you wouldn't chew with your mouth half open like that," his mother said.

He made sure his mouth was closed before continuing.

"Why you didn't want to stop and get a new pair of pants is beyond me," she said, pulling a second slice free from its connective thread of cheese. "Even with the camouflage ones, you're down to two pair. We were right there. Wouldn't have taken but five minutes."

"We can get them anytime," he said. "I just didn't feel like it."

He wasn't about to tell her the real reason. That he'd seen Melissa and her mom inside the store, looking at the girls' stuff. It was a good thing he'd noticed them. It was hard enough buying your clothes in the Big Boys' section, without having Melissa announce it to the world. He could just hear Melissa spilling the beans on Monday: "Saw Toby Saturday night. Buying jeans in the chunky boys' section. Even the dressed-up dummies are fat!"

Mrs. Scudder took another sip of beer and checked her watch. "You won't mind if I just drop you off at home, will you? I'm meeting Doug at the movies. You're welcome to come. You know, he likes you even if you don't like him. I don't know what you've got against him. Sometimes I think any man I'd go out with wouldn't be good enough for you."

Toby figured she was probably right. Then he changed his mind. There had to be somebody out there who wasn't bossy or show-offy or dumb.

"Maybe I'm just looking out for you," he said, only half serious.

She laughed. *"You? Look out for me?"*

He took another bite of his pizza and turned away.

Not often, but sometimes, Toby liked to think of himself as the man of the house. There was only him and Gordon, after all. And even though Gordon was older, anybody with an ounce of sense would know that Gordon didn't give two hoots about anything but money and girls. You'd think a mother would know what was what when it came to her sons.

"How come you and Mr. Fitness stopped going out?" he asked suddenly. "How come you're going out again now?"

"I wish you'd stop calling him that," she said. "You do it just to get on my nerves. His name is Doug. And if you must know, we had a knock-down, drag-out fight when you were at Uncle Kevin's. What can I say . . . he came crawling back."

"What about what's-his-name? You know—" He wanted to say "Black Toe," but changed it to "The other one."

"He's an old, old friend," she said, looking uncomfortable. "That'll never happen again." She took another sip of her beer. "You're sure you don't want to come? Doug said you could. You're always complaining about how there's nothing to do."

"I don't feel like listening to how many sit-ups he can do . . . or how putting butter on your popcorn means you're gonna die before you're twenty."

"Some of what he says is true," she said. "If you watched what you ate a little better, you could lose some weight. You might feel better about yourself."

"I feel fine about myself," Toby said, letting the slice he'd been working on drop to his plate.

How could a person eat with that rotten anchovy smell all around?

□   □   □

That night Toby had the popcorn ready and everything, only to learn that *Saturday Night's Main Event* had been preempted by a variety show. He watched the show long enough to see that it stunk big-time—a bunch of old fogies singing and tapdancing and telling jokes that weren't funny.

He took the popcorn to his room and sat on the bed, watching Slammer and Crusher eat their snack. He'd dropped a pinch of flakes into the bowl, and the fish were hard at it, zipping and darting and lunging. They looked happy and healthy.

For a while there, after the summer camping trip, Toby hadn't known if the fish were going to make it. He still felt guilty about leaving Gordon in charge of feeding them. Gordon hadn't fed the fish even once in three days. By the time Toby got home, the fish were near death . . . pale and hugging the bottom. All eyes. "How?" they seemed to say through the glass. "How could you do this to us?"

Toby had tried explaining to them that he hadn't known Gordon was completely brain dead. He'd suspected it, maybe. But he'd never thought that anyone, even Gordon, could "forget" something so important.

Just thinking about it made Toby mad. Mad at Gordon and mad at his mother for making him go on that stupid backpacking trip with her and Mr. Fitness. As if hiking three miles straight up a trail with thirty pounds on your back could be fun. Toby had used Gordon's old pack. The thing didn't fit at all. The frame was wobbly and the hip buckle was broken. He had to hold the bottom straps together to keep the pack from bouncing and putting even more of a strain on his shoulders. Besides that, it was hot. So hot the sweat just poured off him, plunking steadily into his eyes and carving streambeds down his back.

Except for stopping for lunch, Toby hated every minute of it. By the time they reached the snow-ringed lake, he wanted to fall over in a piece of shade and die. He was about to shed his pack when Doug said, "Not here! I know the perfect site. It's across the way."

So they hiked another half mile in search of the perfect campsite. Then the tents had to be set up. Toby stood there holding one pole after another as mosquitoes the size of Stealth bombers sucked him full of holes. There were flies too. Big, black, and hairy. They seemed to enjoy the back of his neck the best. Their jaws were like pliers. Even when you swatted at them, they'd stay right there, willing to brave death for the chance of ripping out another mouthful of meat.

When the tents were up, it was time to bring in firewood and start dinner. Toby barely had enough energy to eat. He sort of slumped there before the fire, eyes smarting from the smoke. He fell asleep on top of his sleeping bag in the little orange tent without even taking his clothes off—

And woke up freezing and covered with dew, the bites on his wrists and ankles and neck suddenly on fire. His already-bruised shoulders wanted to know why anyone in his right mind would choose to sleep on ground that was rock hard. But the worst of it was, he had to pee.

Struggling out of the tent, Toby wondered where the light switch was. Weren't there supposed to be stars? Didn't stars come with the deal? It was so dark, he couldn't see his hand in front of his face. He stumbled about until he found a spot he thought was far enough away from the tents—relief coming in the nick of time.

Though the mosquitoes and flies had turned in for the night, there were other things out there. Cries and whispers and things rooting around not far from where he stood. A smell came to him. Something foul. Toby finally associated the smell with the image of a cartoon animal . . . black and white, with a French accent. Except this wasn't cartoons! He turned, tripped, and half ran, half crawled his way back to the tent.

He barely slept at all that night, what with all the wild creatures parading through the campsite. By morning the clouds had cleared. He was awakened by the sun, made brighter by the orange of the tent. Still half asleep, he peered out to see Doug charge naked into the lake, screaming when he hit the cold and urging Toby and his mom to join him. Toby heard his mom giggle when Doug came dripping back to shore. "What are the neighbors gonna think?" she said.

Toby spent most of the day in his tent, recuperating. He'd brought a couple of wrestling magazines with him, and he wore out the pages. Later, he greased himself up with half a bottle of insect repellent and tried some fishing. He lost two lures in five minutes.

Mr. Fitness, alias Doug, pranced around most of the time in his boots, hiking shorts, and a *No Pain, No Gain* headband, flexing his muscles and working on his tan. Not that his tan needed any more work. Doug was a roofer. Toby guessed he was one of those guys you always see on roofs—shirtless—keeping an eye out for good-looking women walking by below.

Mrs. Scudder wasn't any more used to the wilderness than Toby was, but she seemed more than happy to play Jane to Doug's Tarzan. She sneaked off now and then to smoke a cigarette, but mostly she was there, hanging on Doug's every word and trying for Camper of the Year.

Toby stayed clear of Mr. Fitness as much as he could. "Your son's a slug," he heard him say. "The kid's twelve going on sixty. Maybe if he lost some of that excess baggage he's carrying around . . ."

Toby looked down when his hand came up empty. He'd finished the whole bowl of popcorn. Only a few charred, unpopped kernels lay stuck to the bottom. Scraping them up, he tossed them into his mouth and licked his buttered fingers.

"See," he told Slammer and Crusher, "it was the pits for me too. It's not like I was having fun while Gordon was starving you."

The fish had finished their snack and were floating near the glass, looking out at Toby as if they understood. Then Slammer made a dash for the opposite wall. And Crusher cut a streak to the bottom. Toby tapped the glass. Usually they'd come at his tap. But not this time. It was as if they were purposefully fanning their tails at him.

"Heck," Toby said. "I would have thrown those lake fish back . . . if I'd caught any."

ELEVEN

The Broughton Student Council ran a school mail service. There were mailboxes set here and there in the hallways, and anybody could write a letter to anybody else and know that the letter would get delivered.

As class rep, Gina handed out the letters in Room 15. "Wow!" she said on Wednesday. "Here's another two for you, Toby. What'd you do, pay that kid to write you?"

There were a few chuckles, but Toby could tell most of his classmates were pretty amazed and jealous that he was getting so many letters from his Kiddie Pal. These two made it a total of six he'd received in only three days.

"The reason *my* pal hasn't sent *me* a letter," Veronica said for all to hear, "is because he doesn't speak English. He's *Russian*. Mom bought me a Russian-English dictionary to use," she added, tapping the little green book on her desk. "It's a good opportunity for learning another language, don't ya know?"

"Mr. Fenning, my pal is *boring*," Leo said. "All he wanted to do on Friday was play with this stupid matchbox car. It was like I was talking to the wall."

"Leo," Mr. Fenning said, "are you familiar with the term 'poetic justice'?"

Leo shook his head. Everybody waited for more, but Mr. Fenning just smiled, looking like he'd just bitten into a double-fudge brownie and was enjoying the taste.

Megan's letters were really only single sheets of paper, folded in half and stapled shut. Toby's name and "Room 15" were on the outside of each, along with stamp drawings in the right-hand corners. The one that said OPEN FRIST had a stamp of a cat's face with long whiskers. The other stamp showed a heart with an arrow going through it.

Toby opened the OPEN FRIST one. A chalk drawing of a rainbow on a piece of black construction paper fell into his hands. The writing on the regular paper was penciled in thick letters that rose from left to right as if climbing a hill: "Dear Toby, Y can't a bike stand up by itself?"

Toby cracked open the second letter and smiled. BECAUSE IT'S TWO TIRED!!!

◻︎   ◻︎   ◻︎

During language, Toby tried thinking of a joke that he could put in a letter to Megan. He figured he'd better send at least one letter before they met again in class on Friday. Remembering how much he liked knock-knock jokes when he was a kid, he racked his brain, but couldn't think of any. Finally he wrote a short note telling about Slammer and Crusher. He didn't say much, only that both fish were orange and white and that Slammer was smaller and faster than Crusher. *They're funny sometimes,* he wrote. *I like them a lot.*

When the recess bell rang, Toby fought past the rest of the kids in his row to be the first to the ball barrel. He reached in and grabbed one of the footballs, then quickly put a check next to his name on the sign-out sheet.

"Hold everything!" Mr. Fenning said, stopping the rush in its tracks. "I've got several names here of people who need to finish last night's math assignment."

Toby stood impatiently, waiting for the list to be read. He knew that his name, for once, wouldn't be called. He and Leo had done their work together during class yesterday. They'd guessed at most of the answers, but at least they'd finished, and had put their papers in the math slot before leaving.

". . . Sarah, Danielle, Chris, Shawn. I think that's it. Everyone else may leave."

The rush was on again. Toby was halfway down the hall, Leo at his side, when he heard his name called.

"Toby!" Mr. Fenning said. "I almost forgot. I need to see you. Leo, you too."

"We did ours," Leo said.

"I know. But I'd like to go over some of the problems with you. From the looks of it, you both need some help with long division."

Leo groaned.

Storming back into the room, Toby kicked the ball barrel, so hard the front of his new sneaker smudged black from the collision. He felt like throwing the football at Mr. Fenning. Instead he slam-dunked it with all his might. "I'm not going over anything," he said.

"You are, or you and I are going down to see the principal," Mr. Fenning said.

"Good!" said Toby. And he was out of the room, slamming the door behind him. He fumed all the way down the hall. And rushed into the office, nearly knocking over Ms. Penrose, the third-grade teacher.

"Hey, what's going on?"

The secretary, Mrs. Snyder, looked up. "Is that any way to behave?" she said.

Toby plopped himself down in one of the chairs near the teachers' mailboxes. He was in the middle of a long curse under his breath when Mr. Fenning came in.

"Toby and I need to see Mrs. Hawkins," he said.

"I should think so," the secretary said. She buzzed Mrs. Hawkins' office.

Arms folded, jaw clenched, Toby felt his eyes start to water. He sucked in a breath. "I hate this school," he said.

In the end, Mrs. Hawkins had Toby sign a contract. He was to work without complaining on his long division during morning recesses for a whole week. If there were no other "outbursts," the contract would be filed away and Toby's mother would not be called in.

That night Toby was watching TV when Gordon came in with his friend Skeeter.

"Toby, baby," Skeeter said. "How's it hanging, bro?"

Skeeter was about six five and thin as a bean. He waited for Gordon to throw him a Coke from the kitchen, then plopped down at the opposite end of the sofa from Toby. When he flipped open the tab, a jet of spray spurted into his face. Toby laughed. Skeeter picked up the pillow beside him and flung it. Ducking, Toby retrieved the pillow and fired back. Then they both had pillows and were clobbering each other, laughing. It was a standoff until Gordon entered the fray . . . he and Skeeter cornering Toby and letting him have it.

"Give up?" Skeeter said.

"Never!" cried Toby, who was laughing so hard he thought he might wet his pants.

"Give up *now?*" Gordon said. He had dropped his own pillow and was holding Toby's arms while Skeeter continued to hammer.

Toby managed to roll to the floor, arms cradling his head for protection. Then Skeeter was tickling him, and Toby couldn't take it anymore. "I give up!" he cried.

"Don't mess with the main men," Skeeter said triumphantly.

Gordon had moved to the window, watching his reflection as he combed his mussed-up hair.

"Anyway," Skeeter said to Gordon's image, "it'll be a blow-out Saturday night. Steve always has the best parties. We gotta bring some beer, though."

"Not a problem," Gordon said, after another comb through. "I've got connections at the store."

"The last time you drank beer," Toby told Gordon, "you threw up all over the basement steps."

"You puked that time?" Skeeter said.

Gordon turned from the window, red-faced. "Would you believe a tub o' lard like that?" he said.

Toby took pleasure in noticing how thin Gordon's hair was. Gordon's hair was fine silk compared to Toby's coarse mop. Andrea had said that if Gordon were a girl, he'd be okay, but being a guy with a father who had gone bald before twenty-five, it didn't look good for him. That was another reason why Toby liked Carl Scudder—because his son, Gordon, was gonna be as bald as one of those baby-bird chicks you see on The Discovery Channel.

"If you weren't so ugly already," Gordon told Toby when Skeeter left, "I'd mess up that face of yours."

"Up yours," Toby said, ducking out of Gordon's reach and running for his room.

Before turning in, Toby opened his life-story book, the pencil falling onto the bed. He was sure there was nothing else to write. He had already told about being born. About his dog-biscuit rattle and the pictures. About his father splitting. There wasn't a whole lot he could remember after that until he'd started school. He remembered kindergarten being a pretty big deal. How his mom had taken him to school, and how the teacher, whose last name sounded like Hamburger, had said everything would be okay, even though Toby had a death grip on his mother's leg.

I was in kindergarten when I found out how being big could be a good thing. There was this kid named Billy Beakin who was always telling me that the wooden blocks were his. For a while I believed him, and when he told me I couldn't play with the blocks, I'd find something else to play with. But I kept watching Billy. And I never saw him take the blocks home. He never had the blocks with him when he got to school in the morning either. So finally when we had workshop one day, which was really playtime, I went for the blocks. Billy said no, they were his. So I pushed him down and sat on him. He cried like I'd stuck a needle in him. And I got in trouble. But I didn't care. Because I learned something important. I think it has something to do with math, or maybe science: If a big kid sits on a little kid, the little kid can't get up.

Toby counted the pages. What he'd written to-night made four all together, front and back. Four pages! And there was still a month to go before the assignment was due. He might do it after all. Might complete all ten pages and be able to say "In your face" when Mr. Fenning collected the books and re-minded Toby of their bargain.

He was about to turn off the light when his mother knocked once and poked her head in. "Hey, how come you're still up?" Toby was surprised. He hadn't heard the car pull in. "Homework," he said, amazed at the truth of it. "Our teacher really lays it on."

She walked to his bed and sat down. "You mean you didn't just now turn off the TV and run in here?"

"Nope."

"I could go out and feel the back of the set."

"Look!" Toby said, grabbing the book and flipping through the beginning pages.

"I'm impressed," she said. "And beat. How's school, anyway?"

"You know."

"I *don't* know."

"Some days are good, others not so great."

"What are you, a lawyer or something? Actually I've been meaning to call your teacher and see what he has to say."

Toby swallowed. "Yeah," he said, trying to sound

enthusiastic. "Maybe you could call next week sometime . . . or the week after. That way Mr. Fenning'll know better about how I'm doing. It's pretty early yet."

He couldn't tell if she bought it or not. If she called school after today's ball-slamming incident, she'd get an earful.

"You know, it seems we hardly see each other," she said. "Why don't we do something fun together this weekend? Just the two of us."

"Sure," he said, glad that school was no longer on her mind.

Getting up, she leaned over and gave him a peck on the temple. It wasn't often that she kissed him, and Toby liked it—even if he was twelve. It made him think about the time he'd been sick and feverish in second grade, his temperature 105. His mother had stayed right by his bed, really worried. She kept rubbing him down with this alcohol stuff that felt cool on his skin. Toby could still remember how she talked to the fever after each rubdown. "You leave my baby alone," she'd say before kissing his forehead.

They each said good night. Then Mrs. Scudder switched off the lamp and left, shutting the door behind her.

The thing about his mother, Toby thought after arranging his pillow, was that she was still there. She hadn't left. It was that simple. At least he *had* a mother.

TWELVE

On Friday Mr. Fenning led the class down to Ms. Lorimer's for another Kiddie Pal project.

Megan was out of her seat and waving to Toby even before he'd made it all the way into the room. Today the pals were to describe and illustrate their own monster. Toby and Megan went to their old place by the class library to work. Megan opened her box of colored marker pens, and Toby said, "Geez . . . how many you got in there?"

"Forty-eight," Megan said proudly.

Each pair had been given a large, white sheet of construction paper. Toby dropped the sheet to the floor; then he and Megan lay down in front of it. The way Mr. Fenning had explained it, they were to create a monster that had body parts from different animals and things . . . the wilder, the better.

"What are we gonna call it?" Toby said, uncapping the black marker pen.

"Monster Maniac!" Megan said right away.

Toby liked that. He wrote it at the top of paper. "Okay," he said. "It's got a head like . . . like a *pincushion.*" He just blurted it out, not knowing where it came from.

"Yeah," Megan screamed. "And eyes like an orangutan."

"An orangutan?" Toby said.

"It's a big ape," Megan said, nodding forcefully. She giggled when Toby drew two big round eyes that he hoped were shaped like those of an ape.

"And a nose like a hippopotamus," Megan said.

Toby let Megan draw the nose, two big nostrils that looked like caves.

They got into it then, Toby coming up with a mouth that spit slug slime, and Megan suggesting ears like corncobs. "And stinky feet, like my daddy's," she said, her nose crinkling, "when he comes home from work and takes his shoes off."

Toby enjoyed the silliness of the assignment. From time to time Megan would sigh at how beautifully ugly their monster was becoming as they gave it a pineapple bellybutton and vampire knees. Toby didn't know what vampire knees looked like, but Megan laughed when he drew two fangs on each leg about where the monster's knees would be.

When Ms. Lorimer said time was up, each pair had to get up and share. Megan waved both hands as if she were stranded on a desert island and Ms. Lorimer were a plane flying overhead. "Okay, Megan," Ms.

Lorimer said. "Let's see what you and Toby came up with."

Somewhat embarrassed, Toby got up. He cleared his throat. "It's called—"

"Monster Maniac!" Megan finished before Toby could get it out, causing the room to erupt with laughter.

And that's how they shared, Toby doing the lead-ins, and Megan finishing each line.

"It's got ears like—"

"Corncobs!"

"And eyes like—"

"An orangutan!"

"And a mouth—"

"That spits slime!"

"With feet like—"

"My daddy's!" said Megan, holding her nose.

Afterward Toby had to admit he'd had a good time. "That Kiddie Pal thing is all right," he told Leo on the way home, as they stopped to fire some chestnuts at the No Motorized Vehicles sign at the edge of the playground.

"For you maybe," Leo said. "That Simon kid is a real blockhead. He wouldn't come up with anything. He said monsters were stupid. All he did was play with his cars again. That's why we didn't have anything to share. I had some real good gross ideas, too."

They were halfway through the park when Toby heard the little cries behind him. "Toby! Wait!

"I want to show you where I live," Megan said, out

of breath when she caught up. "I been looking for you. Every day. Then today I ran around the back to the playground—"

"And you saw me," Toby said, rolling his eyes for Leo's sake.

"Yep, I saw you. And I ran. I'm a good runner. Can I show you where I live, huh, can I?"

Toby looked at Leo. Leo shrugged as if he didn't much care either way.

"Okay," Toby said. "But just this one time."

Toby fired his two remaining chestnuts and started walking, Leo at his side. Megan squeezed in between them. "I'm six, you know. But I'll be seven in June-ly."

"You mean *July*," Leo said.

"Yeah, that's what I said . . . *seven!* That's pretty old, huh?"

"Old," Toby said.

"Ancient," Leo said. "Better watch out. You might become extinct, like the dinosaurs."

"You like dinosaurs?" Megan said. "Me too! 'Cept for the ones with big teeth. They're scary. But the little ones are okay. 'Specially the green ones. I really like the little green ones the best."

Toby wasn't sure he'd even known dinosaurs came in different colors.

It was a bright day. Most of the leaves had fallen from the trees and were dry and crunchy underfoot. Megan plowed through every clump she came to, kicking up a storm of dust. She hummed as she marched, arms swinging, orange pigtails bobbing.

For a second Toby wondered what it'd be like to have a little sister. There were good points, he thought. You could always get a kid sister to do things for you. After all, you'd be bigger. Plus you could outsmart them . . . make deals that would always come out in your favor.

The bad points? Toby figured there were plenty. A younger sister would be all the time hanging around, for one. And tattling, getting you in trouble. Leo certainly didn't think sisters were worth it. He had two. He'd once tried explaining to Toby just what pains they were: "You know when the skin between your toes cracks because you don't dry good enough? Well, that's what they're like."

Megan led them down Thirty-eighth Street in the opposite direction from Toby and Leo's regular route. "This is it!" she said a block and a half later. "That's where I live." She pointed to a not-so-new blue duplex, then grabbed Toby's hand and tugged him around the back, to where a little patch of lawn lay at the foot of two patios separated by a wall.

"Want to see me ride my bike?"

"We gotta go," Toby said.

"Yeah," said Leo, who had a dollar in his pocket to spend at the Texaco.

Megan didn't seem to hear. She dumped her book bag and got on the bike that had been lying collapsed on the patch of grass. She did a couple of quick circles in the tiny parking lot, lifting her hands from the handlebars once and almost losing control.

"You'd better watch out," Toby said, surprised at how much he sounded like some carping parent.

"Come on," Leo said. "Let's split."

Megan braked and tumbled off the bike to one side. The bike clattered to the pavement. Toby turned to go. He looked back when he heard shouting coming from inside one of the two apartments. He checked each of the sliding glass doors that led into the apartments from the little patios, but both doors were curtained. Although the words were loud, they came too fast to make out.

Leo was looking toward the apartments too. "Sounds like a fight," he said.

Toby nodded. He was pretty sure the voices were those of a man and a woman. He strained again to hear, but the whoosh of traffic on the street in front made it all sound like gobbledygook. Toby hoped the voices were coming from the other apartment, not the one that Megan was walking up to after picking up her book bag and slinging it over her shoulder. But he could tell from the way Megan walked, like she had to pull each step up from quicksand, that it probably wasn't so.

The thing that amazed Toby was, Megan never looked back. Never once. Even though she had to know he and Leo were still there. She didn't say goodbye or wave either. Just went up to the door, her shoulders rising and falling in a sigh before shoving open the sliding glass panel just wide enough to slip through. The harsh-sounding voices stopped. Megan stepped inside, the door closing behind her with a shush. In a second the curtains were pulled back by a hand. A man looked out, the anger still visible on his face. Then the curtains shook back into place.

"Must be her old man," Leo said.

Toby nodded.

"She's a neat kid," Leo said. "Wonder if I could work out a trade, get rid of my two bratty sisters for her."

Toby imagined Megan's mom and dad making up, embarrassed that their daughter had come in when they were in the middle of a fight. Then, suddenly, the voices came again, as loud and angry as before, the sound needling the tops of Toby's ears.

"My parents can really go at it too," Leo said.

Toby couldn't help wondering where Megan was, inside the apartment. If she'd gone to her room, or had locked herself in the bathroom. He wondered if she was used to the shouting. If she was scared. Then he just wanted to forget the whole thing.

"You still planning on spending that dollar?" he asked Leo when they'd crossed the street.

"We'll split it down the middle," Leo said.

"Good," said Toby. "I feel like a Charleston Chew."

□   □   □

Toby wished he hadn't seen the news report about Seattle. Well, it wasn't about Seattle, really. It was about the Seahawks football team. But it made him think about Seattle and what had happened over the summer.

In July, Toby had gotten on an Amtrak train bound for Seattle. The invitation to stay with Uncle Kevin and Aunt Rhonda and the boys had come back in May, the same day Toby had been suspended by Mrs. Hawkins for socking Brian Loper. That night his mother had spent a half hour on the phone with her brother. Toby overheard most of what she said.

"I don't know what to do with him. He's mouthing off more than ever. In trouble again at school. . . . He's bigger than I am, for crissakes. He doesn't do a thing around here but mope. . . .

"It might be good for him. Give him some responsibility. You're darn right. Okay, I'll get him."

Uncle Kevin had asked Toby if he wanted to spend some time with them over the summer. He talked about water skiing and taking in a few Mariners games and island hopping on the ferries. "There's a good parks program right down the street—they do summer sports and games and things." He thought Toby could get involved and make some friends doing stuff like that in the mornings. In the afternoons Toby would baby-sit the boys while Aunt Rhonda did some serious job hunting. She planned on working again come fall when Benji started kindergarten.

"Sounds like you and your mom could use a vacation from each other."

Toby had said yes to the whole deal. Yes to getting away from boring old Aspen Street. Yes to putting space between himself and his mother and Gordon. Yes to taking in a couple of Mariners games. Yes to watching his cousins. Especially yes when he remembered Leo would be spending most of the same month in California.

DON'T EVER MENTION FLYING TO A FIVE-YEAR-OLD! Last summer I went to Seattle to baby-sit my two cousins, Nathan and Benji. Benji's the littlest. He's five. And the thing is, they like me. I mean, I think they really do. They were glad I was gonna be living with them for a month and that I was gonna be their sitter in the afternoons.

The first day goes great. We wrestle on the back lawn. I take them to the park and give them a real hard spin on the twirly thing. And Uncle Kevin and Aunt Rhonda are both real pleased when they come home. They don't say anything, but I know that if things work out for the month, they might ask me to stay longer. Like forever, maybe. Who knows? Anything is possible.

The next day everything goes great too. In the morning I meet this kid at the parks program who's kind of big like me and we have a pretty good time playing handball, knocking a tennis ball off this huge concrete wall.

Then on the third day, something crazy happens. Nathan and Benji and I are climbing the big tree in the backyard. Benji's really good at climbing, better than Nathan even though he's younger. We get pretty high up. And I say, "Wouldn't it be nice if people could fly." That's ALL I said! Then Nathan, who's kind of a baby for being eight, starts crying because his foot is stuck in one of the cricks of the tree, and when I turn to see about getting him loose and stopping him from crying, I hear Benji say something about flying. He says, "Wheee!" like he's pretending to fly. But the thing is, he doesn't just pretend! The goofball actually takes off. I look around just in time to see him fall through the air, arms waving, saying "Wheeeeee!"

Then there's yelling and screaming all over the place. Benji ends up breaking a leg and bruising two ribs. And Tobias Scudder is on the next day's train back to Vancouver.

Toby shut the book without even bothering to count the lines.

"*Flying?*" his mother said when she picked him up at the train station. "You were teaching them how to *fly?*"

THIRTEEN

Already, people were talking about Halloween. It was still three weeks away, but on Tuesday Toby brought up the subject of the class party, hoping to keep Mr. Fenning from starting the language lesson.

From his seat in the back, Leo took up the plea. "You can never plan things too soon," he said.

"Right," Josie added. "We'll need time to get the decorations together."

"And to decide on games," said Melissa.

"And refreshments," said Jake.

"You mean we're supposed to have a Halloween party?" Mr. Fenning said, scratching his head. "No one told me."

Flames of outrage shot up like little grass fires here and there, threatening to ignite a full-scale mutiny.

"Okay, okay," Mr. Fenning said. "It's a bit early,

but I guess it can't hurt to be prepared. At least we'll have it out of the way. The class meeting has now begun."

He looked at Toby. "How 'bout coming up and keeping track of who's bringing what?"

Toby shook his head. Handwriting wasn't one of his strong points, and he didn't want people saying, "What? . . . What's that supposed to say? . . . What language is that, anyway?"

"*I'll* do it," Veronica said. "I've done this kind of thing before. And I'll copy it all down on paper when we're *finished*. The way you're *supposed* to do it."

Toby was sure if he let his fingernails grow really long and dragged them hard across the front board, the resulting sound would be a pretty good likeness of Veronica's voice. Mr. Fenning thanked Veronica for volunteering and gestured her forward. Veronica strutted to the front, took up some chalk, and wrote *Refreshments, Games,* and *Music.*

"And decorations!" Josie cried, causing Veronica to erase everything and start over.

Soon the board was filled with who would bring what. Toby thought about volunteering Gordon's boom box for the music part of the party but decided against it. It would be just like Gordon to say "Drop dead" when he asked him. "I'll bring some chips and dip," he said instead. He liked clam dip, and no one ever brought it. Plus he wanted to be sure there were some barbecue chips at the party in case he got hungry watching everybody dance.

About ten kids said they'd bring music tapes. Josie and Melissa decided they'd be in charge of decorating. They asked for helpers, and Luanne and Gina raised their hands.

"Of course we'll need some men on the committee too," Melissa said, looking at Jeremy, whose face turned red as a stop light.

"I guess I could be on it," Jeremy said.

"She said *men*," Toby said.

"That must be why you're not signing up," Jeremy shot back.

The two boys locked stares.

"We're not here to insult each other," Mr. Fenning said. "If we are, we might just as well scrap both the preparation *and* the party."

"I'll be on the committee," Leo said.

Breaking his dagger stare, Toby turned to Leo, who motioned for him to volunteer, too.

"Is that all the *men?*" Veronica said, not without some sarcasm.

"Put me down," Toby said.

Veronica wrote *Tobias*.

"It's *Toby* to you."

She looked at Mr. Fenning. "Shouldn't something as official as this have the person's *real* name?" she said.

"Change it, Veronica," Mr. Fenning said.

"Yeah, *Ick-a!*" said Toby.

□   □   □

Lunch that day was cheese zombies and tomato soup. The zombies were baked in a pan—a thick layer of gluey cheese between a sometimes cakey, sometimes crusty top and bottom. Mr. Williamson, the janitor, hated zombie day. There was a tradition at Broughton of dunking your zombie into your tomato soup. It was a good way of not directly eating the soup, which tasted like watered-down ketchup. With all the dunking, a lot of the soup ended up on the tables. From his place in the lunch line, Toby could see Mr. Williamson near the garbage cans, a wet towel in each hand and a scowl on his face.

"Cuts!" Josie said, squirming her way into line in front of Toby. She took a tray from the stack and set it on the slide rails. "I hate the smell of cooked tomatoes, don't you? . . . Say, what do you have against Jeremy, anyway?"

"He's a nerd," Toby said.

"No he isn't. At least Melissa doesn't think so. She's hot on him."

Toby watched the cook ladle out his soup. Even fresh from the pot, the soup wasn't steaming.

"Anyway," Josie said, "Melissa and I are chairing the decorating committee, and we don't want any trouble."

"Bully for you," Toby said.

Just then Mr. Fenning came up and asked Toby if he'd stop in to see Ms. Blankenship after he finished eating.

"What'd I do now?"

"Don't know," Mr. Fenning said. "But if I were you, I'd be careful. They say school counselors have instruments of torture stored for noontime use. Glad I'm not you."

Jake had picked a limp carrot stick from the bowl in front of him and was waving it around. "Teacher made a funny," he said, when Mr. Fenning left.

"The guy thinks he's on Comedy Central," Toby said.

Since the kindergartners and first and second graders ate lunch early, Toby never got to see Megan in the cafeteria. He thought it was just as well. If they'd had the same lunchtime, Megan might have wanted to play kid sister and sit next to him—talk his ear off.

A boy Toby had never seen before sat down in Toby's usual place. Tray in hand, Toby stood above the kid and gave him his Ultimate Warrior look.

"Oh," the kid said. "Didn't know. I'll just get." He scrambled to his feet, soup sloshing onto his tray as he hurried to another place.

Toby sat down, picked up his zombie, and dunked it into his soup. He saw Leo walking to the condiment table and nodded his support. Leo wasn't going to sit next to Toby today. Today was the day Leo was to try out his plan for sitting next to Luanne. Having helped Leo design the plan, Toby was eager to see if it worked. He bit into his zombie and threw Leo another look of confidence, glad it wasn't him out there.

Moving toward the tables, Leo suddenly stopped,

his head tipping back as if he'd forgotten something. Slowly, he made his way back to the condiment table to put another spoonful of dressing on his salad. Then inched back toward the tables, buying time just as he and Toby had talked about. The plan called for Leo to wait till everyone else had sat down.

The oatmeal cookies were hard as cement again. Toby plunged his into the soup, figuring it couldn't hurt. When he looked up again, Leo was back at the condiments. He was sure Leo's salad must be swimming by now.

Finally, all places along the sixth-grade tables were filled. Leo began moving along and around the long row of tables. It was like playing musical chairs without the music. As he moseyed, Leo kept a watchful eye on Mrs. Zimmerman, who was helping Mr. Williamson sponge up some third grader's soup.

Toby had finished his zombie and was still hungry. Quickly, so as not to miss the rest of the plan, he leaned across the aisle to the next row of tables, informing Lester Carter from Mrs. Wyatt's class that Lester didn't really want the rest of his zombie.

"I put my mouth on it," Lester said. "Here and here."

"So cut the mouth parts off," Toby said. "Geez, Lester, do I have to think of everything?"

By the time Toby was dunking Lester's zombie into what was left of his tomato soup, Mrs. Zimmerman had noticed Leo. Leo was still traveling around the tables, looking confused, like some dazed plane wreck survivor. He timed it perfectly, coming to a stop beside the girls just as Mrs. Zimmerman beelined over.

"Leo, what in the world are you doing?"

"Nothing, Mrs. Zimmerman."

"Well, sit."

"All the places are taken, Mrs. Zimmerman."

"You've been walking in circles for ten minutes. Just sit! Now!"

"But—"

"I said—"

"Okay, okay."

Shrugging his shoulders by way of apology to Luanne and Melissa, and nodding toward the stone-faced Mrs. Zimmerman, Leo squeezed himself between the two girls. As soon as he'd settled in, he looked down at Toby.

Toby gave thumbs up. He watched as Leo happily dunked his zombie only inches away from Luanne, who, Toby now saw, looked like that lady in the air-freshener commercials who discovers an unwanted odor under her kitchen sink.

"You were great!" Toby told Leo after the cafeteria had cleared for recess. "What'd you guys talk about?"

Leo frowned. "Did you know she has an older brother named Butch who's a black belt in karate?"

"How the heck would I know that?" Toby said.

"It's hard to figure about a guy named Butch who's a black belt . . . don't you think?"

"How come you were talking about this guy anyway?" Toby said.

"We didn't start out talking about him. I told her I had her phone number—that I looked at the class list taped to the inside of Mr. Fenning's plan book and wrote down her number. Then I asked if it was okay if I called her sometime."

"And?"

"And she didn't think it was such a great idea. She said if I called, she'd have her brother rub me out. That's how we got talking about Butch."

"Oh," Toby said.

"To tell you the truth," Leo said, "I'm not sure I like her anymore. She doesn't even dunk her zombie —just picks at the insides with her fork."

"Did you tell her how much you like her coyote shirt?"

Leo banged his forehead. "Oh, man . . . I knew I was gonna forget something. No wonder it didn't go right." His face brightened. "Anyway, one neat thing is the plan worked. Worked perfect, didn't it?"

"Two great minds," Toby said. "We're like a tag team. Ricky 'The Dragon' Steamboat and the Texas Tornado."

"Where you going?" Leo said as Toby turned into the main hall instead of heading for the playground doors.

"I'll meet you out there in a minute," Toby said. "Ms. Blankenship wants to see me."

"Trouble?"

"I don't think so." But he couldn't be sure. You couldn't ever be sure of not being in trouble around this place.

He entered the submarine room and found the counselor finishing up a sandwich, the air smelling of egg salad.

"Oh, Toby, good. Come in and sit down. Ms. Lorimer asked me to talk to you. It's about Megan McDaniels, your Kiddie Pal. According to Ms. Lorimer, Megan has really taken to you. She likes you a lot."

"She sends me letters," Toby said. "Or used to. She hasn't sent any since that day she wanted me to see where she lived."

"Did you get to meet her parents that day?"

"No. Why?"

"Just wondering. Her mom and dad have recently separated. Ms. Lorimer says Megan hasn't been herself since the separation. She cries a lot in school. Ms. Lorimer and Megan's mom and I all got together and thought it might be good for Megan if you could walk her home after school for a couple of weeks."

Toby swallowed. He couldn't imagine Megan crying. She was the happiest kid he'd ever known. Even happier than Benji before his flight from the big tree.

"You don't have to mention anything about her parents," Ms. Blankenship said. "She just needs a friend right now. What do you say?"

"Sure," Toby said, thinking Leo wouldn't mind having Megan walk partway home with them for a couple of weeks. "I could walk her home."

"You would?"

"Sure, no sweat."

"Thanks, you're a gem. I'll tell Ms. Lorimer, and she can pass it on to Megan's mom. Mrs. McDaniels wants to meet you first. She's been picking up Megan every day, so if you leave your class a few minutes early this afternoon, you could meet her then. I'll clear it with Mr. Fenning. Tomorrow you could start picking up Megan yourself. Sound okay?"

Toby nodded. He left Ms. Blankenship's office kind of stunned. Stunned because he'd never been asked to do something this adult before. And because Ms. Blankenship had called him a gem. A gem? Him? Toby Scudder?

As he stepped onto the playground that noon recess, Toby felt good. Better than he'd felt in a long time.

He had no way of knowing how quickly things would change.

FOURTEEN

"Fight!" someone yelled. "FIGHT!"

Toby Scudder, Ultimate Warrior, heard the cry. Heard it and felt the commotion around him even as he lunged forward. He couldn't tell if the *Yeah!*s and the *Get 'im!*s were for him or for Jeremy. One second he had his arms clamped around Jeremy in a bear hug, the next he was on the ground, rolling and grunt ing, the grass so close he could taste it.

He ended up on top, breathing hard, using his weight. But the body beneath was like a snake, squiggling, sprouting fists that fired like pistons. Toby jerked from side to side to escape the flurry, teeth gritted. The shouts around him were a blare of un-tuned instruments, harsh and screeching. The fists leaped up at him like giant insects, landing swiftly, leaving their stingers behind. Then Jeremy slipped free and wheeled, and Toby felt the air rush out of him as he was rammed from behind.

Up on his knees, Toby struggled for balance. Then he was down again, rolling to right himself, punching wildly. His nose suddenly burst with pain as Jeremy, too, swung without stopping. Toby's jaw took a shot, his teeth ripping into his tongue. He screamed out, holding his position as best he could, knees pressed into Jeremy's shoulders. Jeremy's grunts came louder as his effort increased. Toby was sent sprawling back as one of Jeremy's swings caught the bone around his eye.

"You jerk!"

"You started it!"

"Did not!"

"Did too!"

And the rolling began again.

Mrs. Zimmerman and two other staff assistants charged onto the scene like police discovering a murder still in progress—eyes flashing, siren-voices wailing. Toby felt the sharp pulls and tugs from behind as, up front, his fingers were peeled from their grip.

"Stop it this instant! Both of you! Are you crazy? STOP!"

Toby was one huge heart, pounding, his legs weak beneath him as he stood. He felt something wet trailing down his chin. The pain around his eye flamed on again, like a trick candle you can't blow out. Jeremy's fists were still clenched and at the ready in front of him, his face streaked with red. Was it blood? Toby hoped it was. Then he saw a thick drop of red splash onto his own shirt. He ran the back of his hand across his nose, felt the liquid and the warmth. Suddenly, one of Jeremy's fisted hands went limp. He cradled it with the other, as if holding an injured bird. "Owww . . . my hand!" His shirt was smeared with grass stains. A splotch of mud hung like a dark moon on his forehead.

"You started it, you jerk!"

"Did not!"

Toby couldn't see for the tears. Everything had gone liquid.

"I can't tell you how much trouble you two are in," Mrs. Zimmerman said. "You could have killed each other! Is that what you wanted?"

The other kids, still gawking, had gone quiet. It was as if they knew. Knew that they'd witnessed the fight of all fights. Through his watery view, Toby could see half the school staring at him. He put his hand up to his eye, the knot of swelling growing even as he touched it. His nose was a tube of red paint drip-dropping onto shirt, pants, his new sneakers.

"A draw," someone called out from the throng. "They fought to a draw!"

"No, Toby had him."

"No way."

"Way."

"Jeremy held his own."

"It's about time somebody took Toby."

Toby turned fiercely to discover the speaker. But the faces blurred and seemed to whirl with the shouts he could still hear in his head. His eye caught fire again. Then he and Jeremy were escorted in—first Jeremy, then Toby. Jeremy jerked his head back, eyes pooled with tears yet still able to spit fire. Toby flung poisonous stare darts of his own.

He was halfway to the office when it hit him. Hit hard. Harder and with a clap of pain worse than any punch to the face. He'd been in a fight. A serious fight. And for the first time in his life, Toby Scudder hadn't won.

          □   □   □

Toby could see the veins and ropy stuff sticking out of Mrs. Hawkins' neck.

"Are you trying to tell me that all this occurred because Brian Loper picked his nose?"

"Yes," Toby said. "I mean . . ." He stopped, realizing how dumb it sounded, and squeezed the wet ball of tissue in his hand before bringing it up to his nose. Dabbing once, he pulled the tissue away and looked at it. The bleeding had stopped. He held the blue ice pack to his eye with his other hand, the cold numbing the pain. "It'll be a shiner for sure," Mrs. Snyder had said. "I don't know about you boys. You're like animals."

Ms. Blankenship entered the office and shut the door behind her. "Your mom's on her way over."

"Any word from the hospital?" Mrs. Hawkins asked.

"Not yet."

The school nurse had accompanied Jeremy to the hospital for X rays of his hand. Toby had heard the discussion from the health room while Jeremy sat in the office only a few feet away, moaning. Jeremy's dad was going to leave work and meet them at the hospital.

"All right, Toby—let's try again," Mrs. Hawkins said. "The truth. From the beginning. We've already heard Jeremy's side of things. Plus we have Mrs. Zimmerman's report, as well as statements from several students who were there."

Toby looked at Ms. Blankenship, who nodded her encouragement. He took a ragged breath, instructing himself not to cry. Then he began, replaying the events as he remembered them.

He'd talked to Ms. Blankenship, then had gone out and joined the game already in progress. Brian caught a pass from Jeremy and ran past Toby, scoring a touchdown. Brian trotted back from the end zone with the ball held show-offy in one hand. His other hand was up to his nose. He could have been wiping some snot away. Or he could actually have had his finger up there, in one of the nostrils. Toby had kicked the ground, mad at himself for falling for Brian's fake. Brian had made a move left, then spun right. Toby didn't know how it could have happened. Brian wasn't even fast. But he'd put on a fake. And it had worked. Brian Loper, of all people!

"You don't have to pick your nose about it," Toby

had said as Brian made his way back upfield. "Just 'cause you scored a touchdown. You diggin' for gold or something?"

"He's a regular Roto-Rooter," Leo said, making Toby laugh even more.

Brian gave the ball to Jeremy so Jeremy could punt the kickoff. Jeremy waited till the two teams lined up opposite each other. But instead of kicking, Jeremy looked straight at Toby. "Brian wasn't picking his nose," he said. "You don't know everything. You're just mad 'cause he faked you out of your shorts."

"He always picks his nose," Toby said, feeling his adrenaline rushing. "Right in class he does it. I see him all the time."

"Well, he wasn't picking his nose just now."

"I say he was."

"You're blind. And a poor sport too."

"Who says?"

"I says."

Toby jumped at the sudden buzz of the intercom.

"And?" Mrs. Hawkins said.

"And then we started fighting," Toby said.

Mrs. Hawkins backed away from the table and went to her desk. "Thank you, send her in."

Toby flashed on his mother's stiff form in the doorway. The black stretch pants. The maroon-and-gold Olympic Lanes windbreaker. The angry eyes.

Mrs. Scudder plopped her purse onto the table and

sat down hard, her eyes boring into Toby. "Why am I not surprised?" she said.

"I think it's best if Toby tells you what happened in his own words," Mrs. Hawkins said. "Toby?"

Toby kept his eyes on the fake wood of the table the whole time.

"And the other boy?" Mrs. Scudder asked Mrs. Hawkins when Toby had finished.

"He's having X rays. His hand may be simply bruised, or he may have broken a bone. One of his teeth was loosened."

"How many times have we talked about this kind of thing!" Mrs. Scudder suddenly let loose in Toby's ear. "You know I don't approve of fighting. What am I going to do with you? Look at you, you're beat up yourself. Maybe you've finally learned your lesson. Have you? Is this what it takes? I'm talking to you! Look at me!"

Toby felt the stinging slap to his shoulder.

Then more swats, starting at the shoulder and moving up, one for each word: *"What—am—I—going —to"*—the last blow striking the back of his hand and the ice pack still in his grasp—*"DO!"*

Her voice caught. The hitting stopped. Toby watched the table's fake grain pitch and roll like waves. Ms. Blankenship cut through the heavy silence. "Toby, why don't you wait outside while we finish up in here."

In the outer office, Toby took the corner chair, the

one that couldn't be seen from the hall. The meeting inside Mrs. Hawkins' office went on forever. When the dismissal bell sounded, Toby crouched even closer to the wall as kids rushed for the front doors, laughing, talking, calling out to one another. He wondered if Ms. Blankenship had told Ms. Lorimer not to expect him. Wondered if Megan and her mom were waiting for him even now. Soon the hallway was quiet again.

Finally, his mother came out, Mrs. Hawkins behind her. His mother's eyes were wet and red. Toby's stomach flip-flopped right there. He wanted to rush up to her and tell her he'd take a hundred more swats, as many as she wanted. "But don't cry," he'd say. "Just don't cry."

"Mr. Fenning is gathering your assignments," Mrs. Hawkins said. "I'll see you Monday morning before school. Both you and Jeremy are suspended for three days."

□   □   □

Late for work, Mrs. Scudder gunned the car home. "It'll all get done, too," she said. "Every last thing your teacher has written down."

A plastic shopping bag loaded with books and a list of missing assignments from the beginning of the year lay at Toby's feet.

"I'm calling Andrea. She can come and take the TV for as long as it takes you to get the work done. Three days or three months. Whatever it takes."

She stopped the car hard in the drive and Toby got out. He was barely in the door when Leo called.

"Boy, what a fight! It's all anyone could talk about. Some kids think it was a draw. But I don't. Then we heard Jeremy had to go to the hospital. Gawd, what a great fight! What'd Mrs. Hawkins say?"

"Suspended," Toby said.

"Who?"

"Me . . . Jeremy."

"Both of you?"

"Listen, Leo, I gotta go. I'm not supposed to be using the phone."

"You sound mad. Are you mad?"

"I just gotta go. I'll talk to you later."

For supper, Toby fixed himself a burger. He held some raw burger over his eye while he cooked, remembering how steak was supposed to be good for shiners.

Andrea came by around seven. She winced when she saw the eye. The bruise had turned a purply black, streaked with mustardy swirls. "Oh, my God—the skin's just peeling off in little balls!" she said, hardly able to look.

Scared, Toby touched around the eye. His fingers came back with tiny red-and-white balls. "It's burger," he said. "We didn't have any steak."

She shuddered. "Mom told me what happened. I'm sorry, Tobe. She also said I *have* to take the TV."

Toby helped her carry the TV out to the car.

"You feel like talking?" Andrea asked as they stood together in the dark of the drive.

Toby shook his head.

Andrea sighed. "Cheer up," she said. "It's not the end of the world, is it?"

"Naw," Toby said. But inside he wasn't so sure. He'd lost. Even if it was a draw, a draw is as bad as a loss when it comes to having respect. Toby was no longer King of the School. Nerdy Jeremy had stood up to him.

"What are you doing, picking zits?" Gordon said when he came home to find Toby standing in front of the bathroom mirror. He gave a long, low whistle when he saw the eye.

Toby squinted through the swelling. He couldn't believe what he was seeing. A full hour had passed since his last check, and the purples and reds and yellows looked worse instead of better. He wondered how long it took black eyes to disappear.

"Let me guess," Gordon said. "Either somebody cleaned your clock or you caught a doorknob in the face. You and Leo trying to peek into the ladies' room at the Texaco again?"

"Get lost."

"Okay, be that way." Gordon stopped at the fridge, then headed for the front room. "Hey, where's the TV?"

"Andrea came and got it."

"What for?"

Toby moved his head from side to side in front of

the mirror, hoping to find an angle that might offer hope. "Mom said I can't watch it. She's making me do schoolwork the whole three days. I got suspended."

"That's great," Gordon said, dripping sarcasm as well as sugar from the doughnut in his hand. "You get in trouble and everyone else has to suffer."

"You hardly ever watch TV anyway," Toby said.

"Maybe 'cause I have more important things to do than sit around and watch a bunch of fat guys pretending to know how to wrestle. . . . Excuse me, I've got a call to make. My harem awaits. And do something with that eye. Like cover it up or something. I'm eating."

□   □   □

NEWSFLASH: Mr. Blaine Kellogg, on hearing of his son's three-day suspension from Broughton Elementary, today met with congressional leaders to discuss overturning the suspension on the grounds that Brian Loper, student nosepicker, is a health hazard and a pain in the butt.

"I think the punishment was too severe," Mr. Kellogg said. "Fighting is wrong, yes, but Tobias should be recognized for bringing a health hazard like Brian Loper to the attention of school authorities."

Upon hearing of his father's actions, Tobias Scudder, Mr. Kellogg's son, said, "Dad, it's not the end of the world. Just come home."

FIFTEEN

Toby had never realized how much he counted on school. On going there. On seeing everyone. Even if the schoolwork sucked and the teachers were always on his case, school was better than staying home. He had three certificates of perfect attendance on his wall to prove it. Now he was home. For three days.

He spent his sentence mostly in the kitchen, books strewn over the table, trying to wade through the mounds of assignments. Moving Slammer and Crusher to the counter for company helped some. But it was as if the clock above the stove had been secretly ordered by Mrs. Hawkins to move two minutes backward for every minute forward. When the clock and the work and the boredom got to be too much, Toby shuffled to the bathroom. The swelling around the eye had gone down, but the color had only deepened. The mustardy swirls had turned a gravy brown, and the reds and purples had joined forces, darkening to the yuck of old motor oil.

No TV, no Leo, no school, no nothing. Even food was denied him. Well, not totally. But who wanted to eat fruit and cheese and carrots and stuff like that? "The only food we're out of is the junk kind," Mrs. Scudder had said when Toby had informed her that the cupboards were bare. "You're not going to sit here and pig out. You've got work to do, which I'll be checking twice a day."

She did check, too. Mornings after her coffee. Then again before she left for work. And she called. Almost every hour she was at work. It was the first time she'd ever made good on her threats to phone and make sure he was there. Toby thought it had something to do with Ms. Blankenship's call. The call had come on Wednesday, Toby's first day in prison. Mrs. Scudder took the phone into the front room, closing the kitchen door behind her. She and the counselor talked for a long time while Toby labeled countries and capitals on a map of Central America. His mother's voice came garbled through the door, sounding a lot like the Spanish names he was writing on the map.

On Friday, Mrs. Scudder left early for work, saying she had to pick up some material at the fabric store. Toby waited till the car was well down the street. It was a little past two o'clock, almost an hour before school let out. He could hustle to the Texaco for a snack and stretch his legs a bit before returning to his cell.

The weather had turned cold, the wind whipping his face as he hunched in his jacket on the way to the station. The lady behind the counter looked at the clock when he came in. "You kids out early today?" she said. Toby pretended he hadn't heard and headed for the snacks. He pulled a Twinkies and a 'Bama pecan pie from the rack and reached into his pocket, only to realize he'd left his money at home on his dresser. His fingers kept searching nonetheless, fumbling through old candy wrappers before touching something smooth and square. He pulled the something out.

Great, he thought. *What can I buy with half of a Pink Pearl eraser?* It was the eraser Megan had given him. He stood there with the eraser in his hand, mad about forgetting the money . . . Megan's tooth marks staring back at him.

Toby put the snacks back on their hangers, his stomach gurgling at its lost treasure. The clerk did a double take as he walked out, checking to see if he'd stuffed his pockets. He'd barely gotten back into the wind when a car pulled up along the nearest line of tanks and he heard his name called.

At first he saw only a woman behind the wheel. Then he noticed the orange pigtails. Megan rolled down her window the rest of the way.

"You stay in the car," the woman said as she got

out. She mouthed "Fill-up" to the clerk in the window and undid the gas cap.

"Mommy picked me up early," Megan said. "We're going to my grandma's. That's my mommy."

Toby had already figured out the woman pumping gas had to be Mrs. McDaniels. She had the same orangy hair as Megan. "Hello," she said before turning her attention back to the pump.

"I never had a black eye," Megan said. "It hurts, huh?"

Toby felt himself blush. He wanted to leave in the worst way. Mrs. McDaniels was staring at him . . . at his eye.

Megan unclipped her seat belt and turned to face the window, propping herself up on her knees. "I know you got in a fight," she said. "That's why you weren't in school today. I had to partner with Veronica and Dimitri. It wasn't that much fun."

She didn't say anything about Ms. Blankenship's plan for Toby to walk her home. Knowing it would never happen now, he wanted to say he was sorry. Instead he wondered if Mrs. McDaniels might be the sort to call school and complain that a suspended student was prowling the streets.

"I don't like fighting," Megan said suddenly. "Or people yelling. It's scary."

Toby recalled the time Megan had showed him where she lived . . . the yelling that had come from behind the sliding glass doors.

Mrs. McDaniels rehitched the pump nozzle and went in to pay.

"But people can still like each other even if they yell," Megan said. "That's what Mommy says. You think so, Toby? You think they can?"

Toby had plunged his hands into his pockets to keep warm. He didn't know about people yelling. His mother yelled. Gordon yelled. Mrs. Hawkins. Everyone seemed to have something to yell about. He'd never thought of yelling being scary, but maybe it was if you were Megan's age.

His fingers touched the eraser, and he pulled it from his pocket. "Remember this?"

"I gave it to you," Megan said, her smile coming back on.

"It's a good eraser," he said. "I use it all the time."

"It's okay if you don't," she said. "It's just a junky eraser."

"All set, honey," Mrs. McDaniels said as she whizzed past Toby on her way back to the car. Megan rearranged her belt, then waved as the car pulled out. Toby waved back, the smell of gas sweeping past him, the eraser still in his hand. When the car had disappeared, he put the eraser back in his pocket. It was just a beat-up eraser, he knew. But he was glad he hadn't fired it up the line that day in the hall. Glad he hadn't tossed it in the wastebasket at home.

Walking across the lot, Toby wondered if Mrs. Mc-

Daniels and Megan were discussing his black eye . . . his getting suspended. Mrs. McDaniels might even request that Ms. Lorimer find another pal for her daughter. "He makes me uncomfortable," she'd say. "Reminds me of a gangster."

Suddenly, he saw kids—mostly little ones, spilling out onto Thirty-eighth Street with moms or dads or in clumps together. Toby knew the older kids always lagged behind, especially on Friday. Still, he didn't want to meet anyone he knew. He ran for home. Hard. Like a gangster.

□   □   □

Andrea brought the TV back on Sunday night and handed Toby a little jar of cream called Disappear. "It works," she said. "I swear by it. I use it on my wrinkles."

"Since when do twenty-year-olds have wrinkles?" Mrs. Scudder said.

"They're there," Andrea said. "I can see them."

Toby thanked Andrea for the cream. He hoped the stuff worked. His stomach had been full of butterflies all weekend just from thinking about going to school and facing everyone.

"Your eye's looking a lot better already," Andrea said. "You really do need a haircut, though. I've got my bag in the car. . . . Mom, why not let him wear his hair the way he wants?"

"I don't care anymore," Mrs. Scudder said. "He

can do what he wants with his hair, just as long as he stays out of trouble and keeps up with his schoolwork. He's all caught up. I checked off the last assignment this afternoon."

Toby nodded for Andrea to get her stuff, thinking a new haircut might help draw attention from his eye. He took one of the kitchen chairs to his room. Then Andrea came in and wrapped a big towel around him. "Still want a tail?"

"Yeah," Toby said. "And a few shave lines . . . real thin."

After that it was *clip-clip, buzz-buzz,* and more *clip-clips.* There was no mirror in the room, so Toby had to sit through the whole thing wondering if Andrea was as good as she claimed. Finally, Andrea pulled a hand mirror from her bag. *"Voilà!"*

Toby had to turn his neck all the way to one side to see the tail. It was about a finger's length long, an inch or so wide. And the three shave lines on each side looked pretty even. "I like it," he said.

"Told you I was good," Andrea said.

Even Mrs. Scudder liked it. Sort of. "I've seen a lot worse," she said.

The next morning Toby was up early. He asked Slammer and Crusher if the Disappear cream had helped his eye, but the fish weren't talking. Actually, Andrea had been right. The eye was looking better. It had gone from black to a sort of rosy red with a gold border. Instead of something out of *Night of the Living Dead,* it now looked more like a bad rash. He hoped people wouldn't think he had ringworm or something disgusting like that.

He put on his Blazers cap, lowering the brim. Then he threw off the hat. Everyone would know he was just trying to hide the eye. Better to have it out in the open. He planned on annihilating anyone who made a crack anyway.

"Hey, great do!" Leo said when he ran out to meet Toby for the walk to school.

Toby waited for Leo's judgment on the eye.

"That's the way mine looked when I got hit by a hardball," Leo said. "Took forever to go away."

Both Toby and Jeremy had to meet with Mrs. Hawkins before going to class. Toby got to the office first. Then Jeremy's dad brought Jeremy in. Jeremy's arm was in a sling. There was a cast around his hand.

"I hope you two can work things out," Jeremy's dad said, eyeing first Toby, then Jeremy. He looked serious but not mean. "You mind yourself," he told Jeremy before leaving.

"You *will* work things out, won't you?" Mrs. Hawkins said.

"I don't even know why we fought," Jeremy said. "I mean, it was like we had to, but I don't know why exactly."

Toby knew why. It was because Jeremy had horned in on his territory.

"I've asked Mr. Fenning to give me daily reports on each of you," Mrs. Hawkins said. "You may go out to recess, but the play fields are off limits for at least a week—obviously longer for you." She motioned to Jeremy's arm. "When do you get the cast off?"

"In three weeks at the most," Jeremy said. "It's just a hairline fracture."

She nodded. "I won't make you two shake hands. Perhaps you'll be able to come to that juncture on your own sometime. I think you might have a lot more in common than you know." Then she led them down to class.

Everyone stared and a wave of whispering rose up when Toby and Jeremy walked in and took their seats. Toby could tell that a lot of the commotion was in reaction to his new haircut, and he was glad he'd gone ahead with it.

"Welcome back," Mr. Fenning said to both boys. He threw a hard stare to the rest of the class, stifling the murmuring.

At recess, everyone crowded around Jeremy to sign his cast. Toby thought it was the pits that black eyes couldn't be signed.

"I can't believe you signed his dumb cast, too," Toby told Leo at lunch. "You some kind of traitor or something?"

"Heck, no," Leo said. "What I wrote was *Better Luck Next Time*. I'm no traitor. You're still the Ultimate Warrior."

By the afternoon, Toby's stomach butterflies had flown off to wherever butterflies go. He figured Mr. Fenning must have threatened everyone with electrocution or something worse, because no one—not even

Brian Loper—said a word about the fight. What he discovered by the end of the day was that things were pretty much the same as when he'd left. Mr. Fenning still assigned far too much work. Veronica was still as bossy as ever. Luanne still had her coyote shirt. Leo was working on another plan to make Luanne fall in love with him. And Brian Loper still picked his nose.

SIXTEEN

Toby was to meet with Ms. Blankenship on a regular basis for a while. "Congratulations," the counselor said when he entered the shower-room-office on Wednesday.

"For what?"

"For getting all that work done when you were home. I talked to your mom yesterday. She's proud of you. Mr. Fenning's pretty happy about it, too."

Toby shrugged.

"You might give yourself a little more credit than that. You could have refused to do the work."

"Yeah, and be grounded for the rest of my life."

"Still, you did something that wasn't easy. You stuck with it. How's it going now that you've been back at school a few days?"

"Okay."

"And you and Jeremy?"

"We stay away from each other. Isn't that what everyone wants?"

"What do *you* want?"

"I just wish he'd never come to Broughton. Everything was fine before that."

"You really think so?"

Toby knew so.

"I'm not sure it was all that fine," Ms. Blankenship said. "You've been in at least one fight every year since I've been at Broughton. Don't blame Jeremy. I think it's about time you looked at Toby."

"*Me?*"

"At your behavior. I think you're a heck of a kid. Deep down you've got a heart of gold. But it's all piled over with having to prove yourself."

Toby was studying the tiles on the floor, counting out squares of three tiles on a side.

"Every one of your teachers has said you have a lot of potential. That you could make something of your life despite the few curve balls you've been thrown."

Curve balls? What did baseball have to do with anything?

"No kid has it easy who doesn't have a father there to talk to and do things with. No kid has it easy when new faces are constantly moving in and out of the family . . . when the only parent has to scrape to make ends meet. I know."

"What do you know?" he said before he could stop

himself. He liked Ms. Blankenship all right. But she was starting to sound like all the other teachers over the years who had sat him down and kept talking on and on until Toby had to block out what they were saying.

"You wouldn't believe how closely your situation resembles mine when I was your age. Of course, I didn't go around beating up people. Girls weren't supposed to do that. But I did make the other girls in my class hate me. I said hurting things and wanted everything to go wrong. I thought if I could hurt people and act like a coot, I'd be important. But for a long while, all I ended up doing was making people hate me. I became a lone wolf. And deep down I hated the fence I'd built around myself. I hated myself worst of all."

Toby imagined a wolf. Alone, somewhere in Alaska. The wolf was howling, standing there on a snowy ridge with its head lifted up toward the sky. "Are we done?" he said when the picture left him.

"Yep . . . except I want you to know I'm sorry that the plan for you to walk Megan home didn't work out. Mrs. McDaniels isn't a mean person. She just thought—"

"She'd rather not take a chance on a big dumb kid who gets into fights," Toby cut in.

"You know that's not true."

He wasn't sure what was true or not. He took a deep breath to steady himself. "I'm leaving."

"I'll need a smile from you first," she said.

She made her nose twitch. Not a single twitch like anyone could do, but one in which the end of her nose kept fluttering . . . like the way Denny Sasser could make his eyeballs vibrate for minutes at a time.

"What can I say?" she said, her nose still pulsating. "I must have been a rabbit in a former life."

Toby felt the smile slip through his defenses. He wondered what Mrs. Hawkins would say if she knew Ms. Blankenship joked around and did silly things when she was supposed to be counseling.

When he got back to class, Gina was handing out mail. "Toby, here," she said.

He took the letter, slid into his seat, and quickly broke through the taped end. He hadn't received a letter from Megan in a long time. He missed her. Missed her jokes.

Unfolding the paper, he saw a picture of three people sitting at a table. On the table were plates and glasses and food. The man had a triangle beard. The woman's orange hair flipped up at the bottom. Their mouths were big open circles and had thick black lines streaming out from them, like they were talking. The little girl between them had orange pigtails. Her mouth was an upside-down U. Several round, purple bubbles covered her face. At first Toby thought the bubbles were freckles. But then he changed his mind. The bubbles were too big for freckles, and one of the them was hooked to the girl's right eye, like a tear.

At the bottom was written: DEAR TOBY, I HATE YELLING!

□　□　□

It was a secret. A secret Toby knew and Leo was eager to hear. "I'm ready," Leo said. "Lay it on me."

They were out at recess, having taken the two swings nearest the girls' four square game. Most of the boys were off choosing teams for soccer. Toby would have liked to be with them, but he and Jeremy were banned from field games until Mrs. Hawkins decided they'd been punished enough. He'd been saving telling Leo about the tradition. With Halloween less than two weeks away, now was the time.

Josie, Melissa, Veronica, and Gina started their game, the big, red ball bounding from square to square. Leo stole a glance at Luanne, who sat with Joelle on the steps. Leo's new plan to get Luanne to like him was to woo her with gifts. Today's gift had been a new blue pencil gripper that smelled of blueberries. Luanne had sniffed the gripper, then tossed it in her desk along with the note reading *Somebody Loves You.*

"It's the best tradition ever invented," Toby said, making his voice sound mysterious. His mood was broken as Jeremy came out of the building, his cast flaming white in the sun.

"Out!" Josie screamed at Melissa, who had taken her eye off the ball to give Jeremy a look of love.

Jeremy headed for the open swing next to Toby. "He must have a death wish," Toby said loud enough for Jeremy to hear.

"Hey, that swing is saved," Leo said.

"I don't see anybody's name on it," Jeremy said. Backing onto the swing, he grabbed the chain with his good hand and rested his cast in his lap, looking off toward the play field, where the soccer game had already started.

Toby did a quick check for adults and saw Mrs. Zimmerman scoping them out from where she stood near the basketball court. He sniffed the air. "Something stinks."

Leo sniffed, too. "I think it's coming from over there," he said, jerking his head in Jeremy's direction.

Jeremy set his jaw and wiggled his bottom even more firmly into the strap of the swing.

"Come on," Leo told Toby. "We've got better things to talk about."

Toby decided Leo was right. He didn't give a rip if Jeremy heard about the tradition or not. The guy was a wimp. So he'd gotten in a few lucky punches during the fight. So what? If Jeremy mentioned the tradition after this, it would just be another reason to pound him in a rematch. Twisting his swing toward Leo, Toby said, "It's a job, see. A job that Devon handed over to me. Last year, after he and Jeff Blomberg did it . . . they passed it on to me. And you," he added. "It takes two."

Leo squinted through the glare of his glasses.

"Get this," Toby continued. "Mrs. Hawkins is a pain in the butt, right?"

"Hemorrhoid city," Leo said with a nod.

"Well," said Toby, "every Halloween someone from Broughton's sixth grade has to sneak over to her place and paper the tree in front of her house."

"Toilet paper?"

"Of course, toilet paper. Last year Mrs. Hawkins came to school the day after and pretended nothing had happened. But it had. Devon and Jeff were giggling all day, and when they took me to Mrs. Hawkins' house after school—there was the tree, wrapped better than any birthday present.

"The kids who know about it think it's high school kids who do it," Toby continued. "They don't know it's a Broughton tradition. They'd never have the courage to do it even if they knew. It's in *our* hands. You up for it?"

Toby could tell from the look on Leo's face that Leo was experiencing something holy. "That," Leo said at last, his voice hushed, "is the most awesome, most fantastic, and best thing ever."

"Two rolls' worth of paper," Toby said. "It has to be done right. It's a big tree."

Jeremy was tracing stuff in the dirt with his foot. Toby couldn't tell if he'd been eavesdropping or not. He raised his voice now, wanting Jeremy to be sure to hear what came next. "You and I are the only ones who know about this," he said. "If word gets out, we'll know who it came from."

Jeremy's foot kicked up a cloud of dust. He gave Toby a look.

"Hi," Mrs. Zimmerman said suddenly, stopping at the swings in the middle of her rounds. "You fellas getting along?"

"Just peachy," Toby said.

"Great," said Leo with a sniff. "Now that the wind has changed direction."

Toby slapped him five.

"I think you boys should put more space between you," Mrs. Zimmerman said.

"We're fine," Jeremy said.

At the sound of the bell, Toby and Leo headed together for the door. "What do you think?" Leo asked. "Angel Soft or Charmin?"

Toby laughed. "Whichever has more sheets," he said.

□   □   □

That night, Gordon informed Toby that he and Skeeter were throwing a party on Halloween night. "You'd better be gone," he said. "It's adult entertainment only."

Toby knew that meant girls and probably booze and who knew what else. "I've already cleared it with Mom," Gordon said. "Maybe you can stay overnight at the gnome's."

"I can't," Toby said, enjoying putting a crimp in Gordon's plans. "It'll be a school night. Leo's mom says no stayovers on school nights."

"Well, you're not gonna be here," Gordon said.

"You didn't really clear it with Mom," Toby said. "You're lying."

"Ask her."

Toby couldn't understand how his mother could be so dense. Gordon's last party had almost destroyed the house.

"I promised her Skeeter and I would clean up," Gordon said. "I don't think she really gives a hoot anyway. She's going out herself. With Doug. To some costume thing downtown."

"With Doug?"

"Who else? He's the heartthrob in her life these days. Don't play dumb. You'd have to be blind not to see what's going on between them." He pointed with his thumb to the ceiling. "I'm just glad my room's in the basement, so I don't have to hear what goes on up there."

"What are you talking about?" Toby said.

"They spend the night together, don't they? You think they're giggling over a game of checkers? You really are thick, aren't you?"

"I just might get sick for Halloween," Toby said. It was hard talking through clenched teeth. "I might get sick and have to stay home when you have your stupid party. You wouldn't be able to do a thing about my being here then."

"*You* not go trick-or-treating?" Gordon said. "That'd be the day."

Toby felt some of the anger move out of him. He

wouldn't admit it to Gordon, but he did love trick-or-treating. He liked everything about Halloween. Dressing up. Taking in oodles of candy. Kids running around town scaring the daylights out of one another. Ghouls and headless horsemen and ax murderers roaming the streets. Christmas was okay, but Halloween was the best. Christmas could be disappointing if you didn't get what you wanted. There was never any disappointment with Halloween. All a guy needed was some fake blood and a set of vampire teeth.

When Gordon went downstairs, Toby ripped open the new box of Screaming Yellow Zonkers he'd promised not to eat all at once, and called Leo.

"Great," Leo said, when he heard about Gordon's party. "We'll get to crash it, right?"

Toby knew why he and Leo got along so well. Their minds worked the same. He popped another handful of Zonkers into his mouth. "I got it all planned," he said. "First we go trick-or-treating, see, and get a ton of treats. Then we get Mrs. Hawkins' tree. Then we crash the party here, to see what Gordon and his goonie friends are up to."

"There'll be girls there, right?" Leo cut in.

"Not girls," Toby said. "Women! We're talking sixteen- and seventeen-year-olds."

He stopped chewing long enough to hear Leo sigh at the thought.

□ □ □

Mom's had her share of boyfriends. The first I can remember was this guy named George. He took me to the zoo. I ate four hot dogs, and ended up throwing up in front of the monkey cages. George didn't last long. Mom said he wasn't her type, and that he couldn't be too smart if he let me eat four zoo hot dogs in one afternoon. (When I got home, Gordon told me the zoo hot dogs come from zoo animals that have kicked the bucket. I got even sicker.)

The next guy I remember was named Roman. He was from some other country. He spoke with an accent. I liked him cause he sounded like Dracula. Then Mom got crazy over this guy named Bert. He was a plumber, and Mom discovered she liked him while the two of them were standing over a busted pipe in the basement. After that it was Roger, who liked to gamble on the horses. Mom kicked him out after she caught him going through her purse. There was this guy, Jack, who was a good cook. He cooked whenever he came over. He had a shaved head. I remember wanting to shave my head to look like Jack, but Mom said Jack probably wasn't going to be around that long (he always left a mess in the kitchen) and I'd probably regret having to wait six months for my hair to grow back.

I don't know much about the last guy, other than he had a black toenail, probably from dropping something on it. Andrea thinks Mom only went out with him to make Doug jealous. Doug is Mom's current heartthrob. I call him Mr. Fitness because he's the kind of guy who flexes and stretches even when you're talking to him. He eats things like spinach salads and wheat germs or whatever that stuff is. Last summer he jumped naked in this ice-cold lake. The guy's pretty warped if you ask me.

SEVENTEEN

Josie made a surprise announcement to the class the next week. "Everyone is invited to my house on Halloween night," she said. "My mom and Veronica's and Melissa's are pitching in for punch and treats. We get to party in the basement, which my dad just redid.

"Everyone's invited," she added. "But we don't want everyone to come. It'd be too crowded."

"Josie, you can't invite people to a party and then hope they don't show up," Mr. Fenning said.

"I can't?"

"Well, what if everyone comes?"

"That's okay. It's a big basement. We could squeeze in if we have to."

"Like sardines," Melissa said.

"Body to body!" Leo called out, prompting blushes from some and whistles from others.

"Another party!" Toby told Leo as they hurried

down the hall at dismissal. "Man, this is gonna be the best Halloween ever."

Leo was just as excited. "Melissa says they're gonna make Josie's laundry room into a *kissing* room," he said. "Josie's buying smelly incense and everything!"

They slowed when they saw Jeremy and Melissa walking together up ahead. Just then Jeremy's brother, from Ms. Lorimer's room, came running up the hall, waving a black cutout bat attached to a string. There was another little boy with him. "See, Jeremy—look what I made. It's a bat."

"I said for you to wait for me outside," Jeremy said.

"You guys gonna kiss? I told Ryan you prob'ly would. He wants to see."

The other little kid nodded fiercely.

Melissa turned the color of a ripe strawberry. "Go!" Jeremy said.

"You think they really make out?" Leo said as Mrs. Childs began shooing people toward the door.

"No way," Toby said. "It's a put-on. Jeremy's a put-on."

Reaching the office, they started for the playground doors as usual. Then Toby stopped. Through the front doors he could see Megan with Mrs. McDaniels. Megan was showing her mom her cutout bat, pulling the string up and down, making the bat dance. Toby thought to go over and say hi, and made a move in that direction.

"Hey, where you going?" Leo said.

"Nowhere," Toby said, changing his mind. It would have sounded dumb to say he wanted to go say hi to his Kiddie Pal.

□   □   □

Halloween was only five days away.

"I can't wait till it's over," Ms. Lorimer told Mr. Fenning when the sixth graders arrived for the weekly project. "They're bonkers. I'll be scraping them off the walls by Wednesday."

The task that day was to write a spooky story. Ms. Lorimer gave each pair a paper with the outline of a haunted house. Toby asked Megan what she wanted to write about, but Megan had other things on her mind.

"A lion!" she said. "I'm gonna be a lion! Mommy's making the costume. It's got spots and everything."

"You sure you're not going to be a leopard?" Toby asked.

"Nope. A lion. With spots."

Toby shrugged.

"You'll come to my house for trick or treat, won't you?" Megan said. "You will, won't you?"

"Gee, Megan, I don't know. I've got a ton of things planned."

"But we're going to give out car'mel corn. I'm helping to make it. And Daddy's coming over and taking me trick-or-treating."

Toby tried to think how he could fit in a visit to

Megan's. He figured Megan's dad would probably take her out early, maybe six or so. He and Leo wouldn't get started till later. Toby always went trick-or-treating later. That's when the real trick-or-treating was done.

"Please, Toby. Please trick-or-treat my house."

"Sure," he said. "I'll make it."

□   □   □

Toby was trying out a new cereal called Float-o's the next morning when his mother shuffled into the kitchen in her slippers and robe. He was surprised to see her up so early on a Saturday.

"It's freezing in here!" she said, reaching for the thermostat.

Toby swallowed his first spoonful of Float-o's and made a face. The stuff had all the taste of cardboard. He scooped out a spoonful of strawberry jam from the jar beside him and tipped it over the bowl. The commercial on TV said the new cereal couldn't be sunk. *Never soggy, always afloat.* The jam landed with a plop, sinking several o's. The aftershock of milky waves took out even more. Toby thought about writing to the company. Maybe they'd send him money to keep quiet about his discovery.

Mrs. Scudder pulled a roast from the freezer. "I forgot to tell you. Doug's coming over for supper tonight. I've already informed Gordon that he *will* be here. And I've invited Andrea. It'll be a real family get-together."

"Since when is Doug part of the family?" Toby said around a second, sweeter, mouthful of soggy cardboard.

"We need to discuss what to wear to the Boo Bash," she said, as if she hadn't heard. She set the roast in a pan. "They're giving out prize money for best costumes. The wackier the better. There's a category for pairs. You can help us with ideas."

"You said it was a family get-together," Toby said. "Mr. Fitness is *not* part of the family."

"Officially, no. Not yet."

"*WHAT?*"

"Oh, don't get yourself into a lather. It's a joke. Doug and I have only talked about it once."

"You *talked* about it?"

"It was mentioned. That's all. Once."

"Well, I can't make it tonight," Toby said. "I've got other plans." He scooped out some more jam and flung it into his bowl, a wave of milk leaping the sides. "Mrs. Betenstein is taking Leo and me and Leo's sisters to the store to get Halloween stuff. She invited me to stay for supper after."

The last part was a lie, but Toby was sure he could get Leo to convince his mother it was a good idea.

"You'll have to take a rain check," Mrs. Scudder said.

"*Why?*"

"Because I said so." She pulled the marker pen from its socket and wrote "Lettuce," "Broccoli," "Velveeta," and "Pie" on the refrigerator noteboard. "Where'd this come from?"

The jam had turned the milk a deeper red. Toby looked up.

"It's a drawing."

"Yours?"

"Mom . . . it's by a first grader! My Kiddie Pal."

"What's a Kiddie Pal?"

He told her. "I don't know why I stuck it there. I just did."

The drawing was held to the front of the refrigerator by a magnet in the shape of the Seattle Space Needle. Toby had bought the magnet in the train station the day he left after Benji's experiment in human flight.

"She's a good drawer. What's her name?"

"Megan."

"I'm going back upstairs for a little," she said.

Toby looked at the Float-o's. Nearly all the o's had sunk. "Don't ever buy this junk again," he said.

"You're the one who picked it out."

She turned to leave, stopping at the top of the basement stairs. "My God," she said. "Gordon snores!"

"It's the air rushing through the emptiness of his head," Toby said.

"Be nice," she said. "And don't forget tonight. Six o'clock."

She left. Toby drank the strawberry milk from the

bowl, then threw the bowl and its mulch of soggy, sunken o's into the sink. His mother hadn't even noticed what Megan had written on her drawing. Hadn't even noticed Megan's bubble tears.

▫   ▫   ▫

NEWSFLASH: Today, company chairman Mr. Blaine Kellogg received by Federal Express a letter from Vancouver, Washington. The letter was with regard to Float-o's, the new, just-released cereal. "They aren't unsinkable," the letter said. "I sunk a whole bowlful, with only two teaspoons of strawberry jam and half a cup of milk." Mr. Kellogg was about to call in his chief cereal engineer when he noticed the name at the bottom of the letter. Ecstatic, he ran a hand through his thick hair and picked up the phone, telling his secretary to cancel everything and to book him a flight to somewhere called Vancouver, WA. "I've found him!" he said. "I've found my son! And stop the production of those stupid Float-o's before we get sued for false advertising."

EIGHTEEN

The parking lot at Toys "R" Us was nearly full. "You'd think it was Christmas," Mrs. Betenstein said. She found a slot in one of the last rows. Leo's sister Katie plowed past Toby when he opened the door.

Mrs. Betenstein held the girls' hands for the long walk to the store. Toby and Leo raced ahead. "You boys be at the checkout counter at five on the nose," Mrs. Betenstein called. She and the girls were going to Costumes. Toby and Leo planned to spend their time in Gadgets 'N' Gore.

Both sides of one whole aisle were full of Halloween gimmicks: body paint, electronic skeletons, witches' heads that lit up and spewed green smoke, fake swords, wigs, dirty-old-man masks, wolfman gloves, vampire teeth, bandages made to look old and bloodied. If there was a heaven, Toby thought, it would have stuff like this to play with and wear. He spent a lot of time weighing cost versus gruesomeness. His purpose was to find just the right combination of things under ten dollars to make him look as disgusting as possible.

His basket was half full when they met Mrs. Betenstein and the girls at the checkout. Leo had only one thing in his hand. A wig. A beauty. Blond and thick and so long it reached clear to his knees.

"Eighteen *dollars!*" Mrs. Betenstein said.

"It's the only thing I want," Leo said. "Look what Katie and Rachel are getting . . . whole costumes! All I want is this one wig." He put it on. It covered nearly all of him.

"You won't be able to see," Mrs. Betenstein said.

"I'll cut holes," Leo said.

"Why would you want to wear a plain wig? What are you supposed to be?"

Leo squeaked some unintelligible chatter through the hair, which didn't help Mrs. Betenstein at all.

"Addams Family! Addams Family!" a little boy yelled from the next checkline over.

"Itt!" Leo said through the hair. "Cousin Itt, from the Addams Family. Geez, Mom."

Mrs. Betenstein chewed the inside of her cheek before finally relenting. Leo was jubilant as they walked back to the car. Toby felt good about his purchases, too. He pictured himself in class, everyone stepping back when they saw him . . . the girls totally grossed out.

"You could call home and say you got diarrhea

and need to camp out in our bathroom," Leo said on the way home. "Your mom would never know."

"Leo!" Mrs. Betenstein said.

"Well, he shouldn't have to eat with someone he can't stand," Leo said. "It's not fair."

"You mind your own. If Toby's mother wants him home for dinner, she must have a reason."

Torture, Toby thought when he saw Doug's Jeep parked in the drive. Andrea's Mazda was at the curb, which made him feel a little better. He thanked Mrs. Betenstein.

"Come over as soon as you're done eating," Leo said.

"*If* your mother gives her permission," Mrs. Betenstein said.

Toby stood on the grass as the car pulled away with Katie and Rachel bobbing up and down in their new princess costumes. Inside, he stashed the bag of Halloween gore in his room, then went to the kitchen. Doug sat at the table, freshly shaven, wearing a sweater, jeans, and deck shoes. No socks.

"Hey, look who's here," Andrea said. "You get a costume?"

"Long time no see," Doug said. He took a sip from his glass. Toby noticed the wine bottle on the counter. His mother had a glass at the stove. She had on the apron that said *Just Eat It.* Her face was rosy from the heat of the stove, or maybe from the wine, Toby thought.

"Gordon, get up here and be sociable," Mrs. Scudder called down the basement steps.

"What?"

"Turn off that music and get up here!"

"What's the purpose of the tail?" Doug said, pointing to Toby's new haircut as Gordon came up.

"So all the girls can pull it," Gordon said.

"The purpose is fashion," Andrea said. She looked at her mother. "Are all males as dense as this one?"

"I'd hate to have something like that hanging from *my* head," Doug said.

"It's not your head, is it?" Toby said.

"You're right about that."

"I've seen a lot worse," Mrs. Scudder said. "They're writing names and drawing pictures and everything else on their heads these days."

"And the shave lines?" Doug asked. "They're fashion too?"

Andrea rolled her eyes at Toby.

"Like not wearing socks when it's forty degrees out," Toby said.

Andrea snickered. Mrs. Scudder gave Toby a look. Doug's eyes narrowed, and Toby could see he'd hit the mark.

The roast was on the burned side. The Velveeta not all the way melted over the broccoli.

"So what are you gonna be—a pirate, or something as dumb?" Gordon asked Toby.

"You'll see," Toby said.

"Candace is having a Halloween thing at the

Quay," Andrea said. "She's renting the back room and having it catered."

"Since when did she become rich?" Mrs. Scudder said.

"Since that Ed guy she was engaged to broke up with her. She hocked the ring."

Doug ate quickly, saying he was starving from a "terrific workout" at the gym.

"The party of the year will be right here in this house," Gordon told Andrea.

"What party?"

"The *party hearty* party," Gordon said. "Skeeter and I are putting it on."

"And to repeat what I've already said," Mrs. Scudder said, "no booze."

"I heard you before. Do I look like an alkie or something?"

"I mean it, or it'll be the last party you ever have here."

Gordon winked at Toby, then said, "Okay, okay—how about a glass of wine now, then?"

Mrs. Scudder looked at Doug, who shrugged and said, "He might as well start drinking responsibly at home. I did when I was his age."

Gordon reached for the wine.

"Just a half glass," Mrs. Scudder said. "You want some, Andrea?"

"Coffee's fine for me."

"Good food, honey," Doug said.

"I know the roast is overdone."

"So's the broccoli," Gordon said, spearing a limp piece with his fork.

"You won't be so quick to complain in a couple years when you're out on your own," Andrea said. "Believe me, I know."

"Two years, right?" Doug said.

"Till freedom rings," Gordon said.

"Then what?"

"The Marines."

"If they'll take him," Toby said, pushing his broccoli aside and going for another spoonful of mashed potatoes.

"*Some*body better take him off my hands," Mrs. Scudder said.

Toby could feel Doug watching him. The potatoes fell in a gob onto his plate.

"You wouldn't believe this new kid we got working with us," Doug said when Toby had forked some potato into his mouth. "The guy must be twenty or twenty-one. Looks like one of those sumo wrestlers. I tried to get him to come with me to the gym. I was gonna give him a free pass and everything. You know what he says to me? He says he doesn't like the smell of gyms. Imagine that. The guy's big as a house and he doesn't like the smell of gyms. He's got two speeds: slow and rock slow. He'll be canned before the month is up."

Toby felt like flinging his plate across the table at Doug. He pictured the potatoes stuck to Doug's clean-shaven face, slowly sliding down his chin. "Mom, pass the butter," he said.

He dropped a thick knifeful of butter on the potatoes and mashed it in. When he looked up, he saw Doug shaking his head.

"Hey, don't turn into a balloon for my sake," Doug said.

"You never put extra butter on my potatoes," Mrs. Scudder said. "You say they're just right."

"He's mad," Gordon said.

"Hey, don't get me wrong," Doug said. "I didn't tell about that guy 'cause of you."

Toby took another forkful of butter and glommed it into the potatoes.

"Gosh, this is fun," Gordon said. "Remind me to be here for dinner more often."

Toby forced himself to eat every last bite of potatoes.

Doug asked for ideas on what he and Mrs. Scudder should wear to the Boo Bash. "We want to win the pairs award," he said. "It's worth two hundred fifty dollars."

"Yeah, you guys," Mrs. Scudder said as she cut the pie. "Help us out. Think of a winner."

"Pairs?" Gordon said. "Like Popeye and Olive Oyl?"

Toby laughed. Popeye would be right up Doug's alley. He could flex himself silly.

"I've thought of Bonnie and Clyde," Doug said.

Toby refused to take the piece of pie Andrea handed him.

"How 'bout you, Toby?" Mrs. Scudder said. "Any ideas?"

Toby pushed himself from the table, taking his plate and dumping it in the sink. "All I can think of is Tarzan and Jane," he said with a straight face.

Andrea burst out laughing.

"That means we'd have to go half naked," Mrs. Scudder said. "We'd freeze."

"Not the best time of year for a loincloth," Doug said. "Would be different, though."

"I promised Leo I'd be at his house by seven," Toby said.

"I gotta split too," Gordon said. "Heavy date tonight."

"Wait!" Andrea said. "I brought my camera. I'll use the timer to get us all in." She brought in a TV tray from the front room, set the camera on it, and positioned everyone around the table as she looked through the lens. Then she set the timer and ran into the frame. "Smile, all!" she said.

Toby didn't smile. Nor did he wait for permission to leave after the picture. He'd put in his appearance at the big family get-together. Now he was a free man. Hurrying to the front room, he grabbed his jacket from the sofa.

"You could at least say good-bye, Toby," Mrs. Scudder called from the kitchen.

"Good-bye, Toby," he said.

172 □

NINETEEN

The decorating committee met after school on Tuesday. Luanne was the only member missing. "I think she had a dentist appointment," Veronica said. "Prob'ly her overbite."

Leo had left a pink rose in a little green vase on Luanne's desk before school that morning. It was still there. "She must have forgotten to take it home," he told Toby as Josie and Melissa unpacked the decorations.

Mr. Fenning sat at his desk correcting papers while everyone strung orange and black streamers across the ceiling, standing atop desks and weaving the streamers loosely over and under the lights. At one point Toby and Jeremy found themselves standing side by side. Jumping up to toss a black streamer over the lights, Jeremy suddenly lost his balance. His arms did the backstroke as he struggled to keep his footing on the edge of the desk. Without thinking,

Toby reached out, and Jeremy grabbed hold with his good hand, righting himself.

"Thanks," Jeremy said. "It's this dumb cast. It's got me all out of whack."

Toby pulled back his hand as if he'd touched something slimy. If he'd had time to think about it, he would have just let Jeremy fall.

After the streamers, there were plastic witches and rubber bats to hang. They used fishing line that was almost invisible, securing it to the lights so that the witches and bats appeared to be really flying. It was Leo's idea to let the skeletons and spiders hang even lower so that people would have to duck under them the next day when they went for their seats.

"The other kids are gonna love it!" Josie said when they'd finished. She started a raft of high fives.

"Ouch," Denny said when Jeremy's cast bonked against his wrist bone.

"I'll be glad when this stupid thing comes off," Jeremy said. "Dad says I should save it, because everyone has signed it and it's good to have souvenirs from different times in your life."

"Everybody didn't sign it," Toby said. "I didn't."

"Why don't you?" Mr. Fenning put in. "That way Jeremy will have a keepsake that includes everyone." He took a black felt pen from his shirt pocket and held it out.

Toby looked at Leo. He'd already told Leo about his plans for a rematch with Jeremy as soon as Jeremy's cast was off. "Sure," he said, "I'll sign it." He took the pen and wrote *T.Scudder Ult.War.* in the little white space still left near Jeremy's knuckles.

Gina made a test run down one of the aisles, pushing skeletons and spiders away from her face. "Great idea, Leo," she said. "It's like going through a spooky forest."

"Okay, folks," Mr. Fenning said, "time to go home to our mommies and daddies."

Leo ran to Luanne's desk and picked up the pink rose and little green vase. "You better take this," he said, catching up to Gina in the hall. "It'll need water."

Gina put the petals to her nose and took a good sniff. "Yeah," she said. "Good idea."

□ □ □

Toby always had trouble sleeping before a big day. That night he woke up three times, turning on the light and lying on his side to watch Slammer and Crusher until his eyes got heavy again. There was a lot to think about. Was his costume good enough? Had he remembered to pack everything? Was Josie really turning her laundry room into a kissing room?

Mr. Fenning's suspenders were a big hit the next day. They were orange and patterned with black witches and jack-o'-lanterns. All the kids had their costumes in paper bags beside their desks. The back table was loaded with food for the party. Three kids had brought boom boxes, and there was a lot of shouting as they compared tape collections before the bell rang.

Toby kept his eyes on the clock after lunch, waiting for the social studies lesson to be over so the dressing up and partying could begin. He was already wearing a black sweatshirt and black jeans. In his costume bag were a set of fang teeth, a couple of ratty-looking bandages, a torn-up T-shirt, some tooth black, and two tubes of "blood." His most prized accessory was a scalp mask with a real-looking hatchet imbedded in the center.

"Okay," Mr. Fenning said at last. "Let the festivities begin!"

Toby rushed out along with everyone else. The boys' room became an instant madhouse as the transformations took place. Jake turned into a bum, Chris a Ninja. Denny slid on a Seahawks helmet and cinched up a real set of shoulder pads he'd borrowed from his brother. Michael Adams put bumps of brown paint on his face and neck and hands and said he was a kid with chicken pox.

Leo, of course, was Cousin Itt. His wig came down well below his jeans shorts, so besides his glasses— the lenses looking out from a sea of shag—all you could see was hair, bare legs, and tennis shoes. Jeremy was Tom Sawyer. He'd put on baggy overalls that had about a hundred patches on them. A few guys complained when he took off his shoes and socks, but he only laughed. A floppy straw hat, corncob pipe, and slingshot completed his costume.

Toby slipped the torn-up T-shirt over his black sweatshirt. Then wrapped the ratty bandages over his pants. "Cool," Jake said when Toby put on his hatchet scalp mask. Standing before the mirror, Toby dripped blood onto the scalp, sliming it over his temples and down his cheeks. He blackened his real teeth, put on his fang set, and smiled.

"Youlookterrible!" Leo said in Cousin Itt talk.

Toby thanked him.

The boys were done before the girls, and they helped Mr. Fenning set up the food table and clear the desks from the middle of the room so there'd be space for dancing and games.

Josie and Melissa caused a stir when they came in dressed as babies. "We're twins," Josie said, shaking a rattle. They wore skimpy white tank tops, and diapers over short shorts. Their bonnets teetered on their heads the way babies' do. They had on these huge moose slippers and, for a while, spoke only in baby talk.

Soon the room was filled with mummies, ghosts, assorted ballplayers, a nurse, three witches, and a few Draculas and wolfmen. The primary kids were to serpentine through the upper-grade rooms, and when the kindergartners showed up, Mr. Fenning turned off the lights and told everyone to sit down. Next came Ms. Lorimer's class. Toby couldn't believe how great

Megan's lion costume was. The spotted-fur suit had a hood, a ropy tail, and a big, fluffy mane around the neck. The rubber nose mask had long bristly hairs. Giggling, Megan went right up to Toby's desk. "ROAR!" she said. Then, as if Toby would have no idea who it could be, she said, "Toby . . . it's me, Megan!"

Toby had thought she might be afraid of his costume. But she wasn't. "I know that's not real blood," she said. Then, looking at the fake hatchet blade plunged into the top of his head, she said, "Bet you got a headache!"

The party was a pig out, the music loud. Toby ate most of the clam dip and barbecue chips he'd brought, as well as a half dozen cookies and several glasses of cider. The boys mostly clowned around while the girls danced. Leo talked in his Cousin Itt chatter and sort of floated around the dance floor, swinging his hair.

It wasn't until the end, when Mr. Fenning had everyone help with the cleanup, that Jeremy told Toby and Leo he wanted to be part of the TP-ing that night at Mrs. Hawkins'.

"What are you talking about?" Toby said.

"You know," Jeremy whispered, "the tradition thing." Loose straws from his hat bounced in front of his eyes. "Okay, so I heard you guys on the swings. But you knew I was there."

"You haven't got the guts," Toby said.

"Do too. I've got to take my brother out trick-

or-treating. But between that and Josie's party, I'm free."

Toby did some quick thinking. He figured if Jeremy didn't show, it would prove just what a wimp he was. If he did show and chickened out at the last minute, that would be even better. And if Mrs. Hawkins were to catch them . . . well, when getting caught at anything, it was always better to have more people involved.

"We'll be at Mrs. Hawkins' at eight," Toby said.

Jeremy sucked on his corncob pipe and nodded.

Leo shook his hair. "Bethereorbeanerd," he said.

□   □   □

It was well past four when Toby got home from school. He and Leo had taken their time, going over plans.

"I need to know exactly what you're doing tonight and what time you'll be home," Mrs. Scudder said when Toby came in the back door.

Gordon and Skeeter were packing cans of pop into the fridge. On the table were scads of chips and pretzels and other treats.

Toby told about trick-or-treating and Josie's party. "I think the party gets over at ten-thirty," he said.

"Ten-*thirty?*" Gordon said. "Mom, tell him not to come home so early. Everyone will still be here. He can go to Leo's."

"He's coming home, where he belongs," Mrs.

Scudder said. "He's got a room of his own. He won't bother you. Besides, you guys will be winding down by that time anyway. It's a school night."

"It's Halloween!" Gordon said.

"I've let Mr. Caruthers next door know what's going on," she said. "You know how he complains when he doesn't get warned about extra noise. I also gave him the number of the Red Lion downtown. That's where Doug and I are gonna be."

"That old fart Caruthers'll call as soon as we put the music on," Gordon said.

"Keep it low and he won't," she said. "I'm leaving now. Doug and I are getting ready together. You watch yourselves tonight. Stay out of trouble."

Skeeter took his head out of the refrigerator. "Don't worry, Mrs. Scudder. We're just gonna have some good clean fun."

"Hah!" Toby said, causing Gordon to give him a look.

Mrs. Scudder left with a shopping bag full of costume stuff. She and Doug had decided to go to the Boo Bash as Fred and Wilma Flintstone. Toby thought Doug would be a natural at playing a stone-age dumbbell. Doug was going to wear a geeky, fat tie he'd found at the Salvation Army, and had bought an oversized plastic bat to carry. Mrs. Scudder had already practiced putting her hair into a Wilma ponytail, and had strung together a clunky necklace from chestnuts. They'd rented leopard-skin outfits from a costume shop and planned to wear sandals. When Toby had answered the phone the night before, he'd been greeted with Doug's horrible imitation of "Yaba-Daba-Doo." "My mom says I'm not supposed to talk to strangers," he'd said before hanging up.

Toby redid his costume after finishing off the chips left over from school. Gordon and Skeeter were downstairs making dance tapes when Leo showed up in his wig at exactly six-thirty as planned. He was wearing long pants, but the hair covered most of them. "Sowhere'rethebabes?" he said.

"It'll be perfect," Toby said. His face and scalp mask were freshly bloodied. "Mom says Gordon has to let me in no matter what after Josie's. Gordon and Skeeter can't throw us out. It's like we're invited."

"Got your Charmin?" Leo said.

Toby checked his bag to make sure. Then went to his room to say good-bye to Slammer and Crusher. "It might get loud," he said, dropping in some flakes. "Just stay cool." He picked up the sign he'd made, which read "OFF LIMITS BY ORDER OF TOBY, UL-TIMATE WARRIOR," and tacked it to the front of his door, wishing he had a padlock.

Outside, it was cold and windy. Stacks of clouds blocked any stars from getting through. Toby didn't mind the cold and wind. Even a little rain would be all right; it would add to the spookiness of the night.

They headed straight for the rich people's houses at the new development, passing groups of kids—the little ones with their parents, the rest in pairs or small groups. Goblins, weird painted cardboard boxes with legs, every cartoon and TV character you could name, were out on the street.

It was a long walk but worth it. After an hour, their bags were jammed with top-of-the-line treats: Cadbury's bars, Almond Rocas, even miniature tins of butter cookies. Most of the people who answered the door had the same response. First they drew back, horrified, when they saw Toby. Then they'd look at Leo and say, "What in the world are you?"

"Anybodywithabrainwouldknow," Leo would say, so fast no one could make it out.

Finally, they headed back toward the Broughton neighborhood and Mrs. Hawkins'. "I'll bet Jeremy doesn't even know where she lives," Leo said.

"That'll be his excuse tomorrow," Toby said. "Guys like Jeremy always have excuses."

Mrs. Hawkins lived in a tidy-looking house with a picket fence and a two-car garage in the middle of the block on Stanton Street. The tree, a big maple, spread its branches over the whole of the front yard. As they approached, they heard a *Pfssst!*

"It's me . . . Jeremy," came the whisper.

A shadow with a floppy top came out of the bushes and grew a face when it entered the splotch of light from the streetlamp.

"You better have your own TP," Toby said, mad that Jeremy had showed.

"Never go anywhere without it," Jeremy said.

The house was set way back, so you couldn't see it unless you were right in front. But when Toby and

Leo and Jeremy passed the thick hedge that bordered the property, all three stopped in their tracks.

"Howdy, boys, care to join us?" Mrs. Hawkins called out. She tossed half a roll of toilet paper into the branches of the big maple, which was already striped with paper. Mr. Hawkins laughed, waiting for the roll to bounce down. He caught it, then sent it up again.

"We do this every year," Mrs. Hawkins said. "It's a tradition."

"But—" said Toby.

"Last year Devon and Jeff helped us," she continued.

"You wouldn't believe it," Mr. Hawkins said. "Those boys last year had brought their own paper. Don't suppose you boys have any paper handy?"

"Who, us?" Toby said.

"Weneverhavethatkindofthing," Leo said.

Jeremy clamped his trick-or-treat bag closed. "Why would we bring paper?"

"Just a hunch," Mrs. Hawkins said. "Anyway, come up to the porch and I'll give you your treats."

The boys walked sheepishly up to the porch. They took the treats from Mrs. Hawkins with their hands, unwilling to open their bags.

"Have a good night," Mr. Hawkins said as he tossed up another stream of paper.

"That Devon," Toby said angrily as they hurried off. "What a liar. They didn't get the tree at all. It was gotten for them."

"Well, we would have done it," Leo said, looking up into the light drizzle that had begun to fall. "No question."

Toby agreed. "Of course we would have."

"And I was there for it," Jeremy said. "You said I wouldn't be, but I was."

"Hey, my wig's gonna friz," Leo said, as the rain came harder.

Toby raised his head to catch some of the wet, thinking the blood on his face would look even worse if it ran.

"Let's go to Josie's," Leo said. "I got enough candy to last me a week. Everyone should be getting there now."

"What about Megan?" Toby said, suddenly re-membering his promise. "I told her I'd trick-or-treat her house. She's looking forward to it."

"She's probably in sugar heaven," Leo said. "She'll never remember."

It was a real downpour now, and they took shelter under a tree, the drops machine-gunning Toby's rub-ber hatchet and scalp. Toby was sorry he'd promised Megan. He thought he should have known better. *Things happen on Halloween. It's not a night for mak-ing promises to visit little kids.*

"Come on, man," Leo said. "My hair's getting soaked."

"I've got an extra hat," Jeremy said. "My mom made me take a ski cap just in case it got real cold."

He pulled a ski cap from his pocket, and Leo

tugged it on over his wig. Toby sighed, recalling Megan's excitement during the serpentine. How she'd just about bubbled over at the end, saying "See ya tonight, Toby!" like she was really counting on it.

He sighed again. "Listen, I'll meet you over at Josie's."

"You're really *going?*" Leo said.

"It won't take long," Toby said, still mad at himself for making such a stupid promise. "I'll run the whole way."

He watched Leo and Jeremy take off in the direction of Josie's house, then sprinted for Megan's, thinking the whole thing wouldn't take more than twenty minutes if he hurried.

He was on Thirty-eighth, four blocks from Megan's, when he saw something running toward him. It was small and gave out little shrieks. Like a dog, yelping, chasing something. But as the creature drew closer, Toby saw it wasn't a dog at all. It was a lion. It was—

"Megan!"

Megan recognized the voice and headed straight for Toby, sobbing and burrowing her nose mask and mane into Toby's chest.

"Don't make me go back!" she screamed, her breath catching between sobs. "Oh, Toby . . . please . . . I never want to go back!"

TWENTY

Cars roared past on the street, their headlights turning the pavement puddles on, off. Toby bent down, his arms clasped around the wet, fuzzy cloth of Megan's costume. Other than Benji, when he hit the ground last summer, Toby had never heard anyone cry so loud, so hard.

"Megan, don't . . . Geez . . . Tell me what happened."

The girl pulled back, gasping for air. "Daddy—he was s'posed to take me trick-or-treating—but he was late—and they started fighting—him and Mommy—and—"

"And what, Megan? What?"

She gave out a soft puppy whine, the rain pattering her rubber nose mask.

"Then Daddy threw the plant . . . and the window crashed . . . and Mommy started screaming and crying . . . and Daddy hit the wall with his fist and said he's never coming back. He's never coming b—"

She burst into tears, her head finding his chest again, the last word lost. Toby could feel her heart beating. He wondered how a heart could beat so fast. "We gotta get out of the rain," he said. "Away from the street."

"No!" she cried, her fists thumping his shoulders. "Don't take me back! Don't, Toby!"

He had to think. Think what to do. Josie's party flashed through his mind. The party he was missing. But he let it go. There was Megan. Here. Now. And Mrs. McDaniels. She must be sick with worry. Maybe she was already driving the streets, looking. Maybe she had already called the police. He took Megan's hand and started walking in the direction he'd come from, the girl's sobs softening.

The Texaco station was closed, a single floodlamp beaming from the roof, lighting the rain as it drove on a slant to the blacktop. The phone booth was around to the side, near the restrooms. Toby had used the phone plenty of times. Leo, too. Mostly to call home with fake excuses for why they'd be late, or to get permission to stay at each other's houses.

"We have to call your mother," he said, nudging Megan into the booth.

"No!" she said. "I hate her! And Daddy, too!"

"But we have to. She'll want to know you're all right."

□ 187

He squeezed in next to her and closed the door. For a second he thought how ridiculous it must look: A spotted lion and a guy with a hatchet sticking out of his head, both drenched, stuffed in a phone booth, their breath steaming up the walls.

"We'll just call and tell her you're okay. Maybe you'll want to go home later. In the meantime . . ." He wasn't used to this. To thinking so fast. To having someone else to worry about. "I don't know. We'll think of something."

Even as he reached into his pocket for the quarter, he knew it wasn't there. Why bother bringing money on Halloween? A person wasn't about to get a snack attack on Halloween. "Dammit!" he said.

She looked up, frightened.

"I mean, I don't have a quarter. Do you?"

In the end, he took her to his house. Hand in hand they walked, through the rain, with the wind blowing colder and a few late trick-or-treaters ducking into cars, where grown-ups waited behind whizzing wiper blades.

Aspen Street was lined with cars on either side. You could hear the music half a block away. Four or five kids were hanging out on the porch, smoking cigarettes and drinking beer.

"Hey, you two are a little young for a party like this, aren't you?" one of the boys said when Toby and Megan were halfway up the front walk.

"I live here," Toby said.

"*You're* Gordon's brother?" a girl said.

"Gordon should be grateful he missed the ugly genes," the boy said, the others erupting in laughter.

Toby felt Megan's hand tighten around his. She was probably scared. Probably never seen such big jerks hanging out. Or heard such loud music. He had to stuff his anger down . . . like stuffing socks into his already-crowded T-shirt-and-underwear drawer. He led Megan to the side of the house, stopping under the crabapple tree, the branches thick enough to hold back some of the rain.

"You don't need to be scared," he told her. "I'm gonna come right back, you hear? I'm just gonna go in and call your mom, and then you and me . . . we'll do something . . . go trick-or-treating, maybe . . . it's still not too late. Okay?"

She nodded, pulling off her mask, sniffling up the wet from her nose. Reaching inside his plastic treat bag, he tore off a bunch of paper from the still-new roll of Charmin. "Here," he said.

She took the paper and wiped it across her face.

"Eat some candy," he said. "I'll be right back."

He tore the hatchet mask off his head, letting it drop to the ground, and rushed past the dopes on the porch.

Inside, the place was a shambles. Talk and laughter, voices cranked high. There were people everywhere. A few wearing costumes, most not. His gaze swept the front room for Gordon and came up empty. He had to push his way to the kitchen, where a girl wearing a cowboy hat was on the phone.

"I need to use the phone," he said, almost screaming to be heard over the noise.

"Just a sec."

"No, not in a sec—NOW!"

"Hey, why'd you do that?" she said. She started to
redial. "Somebody get this twerp outta here. He hung
me up right in the middle of my call."

Toby felt the hand clamp down on the back of his
neck. "You'll have to wait your turn," some guy said.
"Now beat it."

He was thrown back into the front room. And now
it was Toby who was crying. Not the sobbing kind.
Not a huge rush of tears. Just a steady, quiet stream
of wet, caused by frustration and not knowing what
to do. When he reached his room, he saw that the door
was closed, the "OFF LIMITS" sign gone. He opened
the door quickly. The first thing he noticed was that
the lamp had been moved from the nightstand to the
floor. Blocked by the bed, it gave off only a dim, shad-
owy light.

"This bed's taken" came a sleepy voice. "Try upstairs or the basement." The voice was familiar. "I
said this room is tak— Toby?"

It was Skeeter, on the bed with a girl. Toby could
see their shoes lying in a heap on the floor. The girl
turned suddenly to face the wall, pulling at her
blouse.

"For crying out loud, Toby, beat it!"

The room reeked of beer smell. Now that his eyes
had adjusted, Toby could see there were cans lying all

190 □

around. The hopelessness of doing anything about it came crashing down on him. He wanted to leave. It wasn't his room anymore. For a moment he couldn't remember what he'd come there for. Then he ran to the closet.

"*Skeet*-er!" the girl cried.

"Get lost, Tobe," Skeeter said. "Last warnin'."

Toby was half inside the closet, rummaging through the pockets of the camouflage pants that hung from a nail on the inside wall. "A lousy, miserable quarter," he said, the sting coming back to his throat.

"If it's just a damn quarter you want," Skeeter said, squirming on the bed. He tossed the quarter and Toby caught it.

Turning to leave, Toby saw the fishbowl, and was surprised he hadn't thought to check on Slammer and Crusher. It wasn't so much the bowl as the beer can that caught his attention. The can was on the nightstand, beside the bowl. He looked harder. At the bowl. The water. There were no darting streaks of orange. And the water was different. Not clear. He thought maybe it was the lamp from the floor making the water look so yellow. He felt his stomach sink even before he got to the bowl.

"I had nothing to do with that," Skeeter said. "They were already dead when we got in here. Somebody must have—"

Toby blocked out Skeeter's noise. He saw Slammer and Crusher near the bottom of the bowl, floating just above the gravel, still. It took him a few seconds to believe it. Then he couldn't see right for the tears that pressed out. He had to force the ball from his throat. "You're idiots!" he screamed. "All of you!"

He lunged for the bowl, thinking if he got Slammer and Crusher outside, they would start to move again. That they'd be alive again. Then he and Slammer and Crusher and Megan could go as far away as possible from this stupid house. Away from the smell of beer and cigarette smoke and the pounding music and laughter and the two idiots whispering over there, waiting to get back to groping each other on his bed.

Away.

□   □   □

They buried Slammer and Crusher under the crab-apple tree. The ground was soft from the rain, and Toby used a rock to scrape out a hole, stopping now and then so Megan could use her tiny hands to scoop out the dirt. When Megan had asked how the fish had died, Toby had lied and said he didn't know, but that they had to bury them. "Like a funeral?" Megan said. "Yeah," Toby said.

Before he set the fish in the hole, Toby said good-bye. First to Slammer. Then Crusher. Holding each in his hand and speaking low to them. Saying he was sorry. "So sorry." Then he laid them gently down, and together he and Megan moved the dirt back into place.

"Shouldn't we say a prayer?" Megan asked.

Toby felt as if all the energy had been drained from him. Did he know any prayers? "You say one," he said.

So Megan did. "Now I lay me down to sleep . . ." she began. And when she'd finished, Toby said goodbye one more time in his head, thinking this couldn't be happening, this couldn't have happened.

Standing, he wiped his eyes clear and took Megan's hand. "We have to go back to the Texaco to call," he said. Megan didn't resist.

Mrs. McDaniels screamed with relief when Toby told her Megan was all right. She wanted to drive right down to the station, but Toby said she didn't have to do that. "We'll just walk," he said. "It's stopped raining."

"I have to take you home," he told Megan after he'd hung up. "You know that, right?"

She looked away. "Is Mommy mad?"

"I don't think so. She wants you back."

As they neared the duplex, Toby realized he was still carrying his treat bag. "You never got to go," he said, holding it out for her to take. "I've got plenty of other stuff at home."

Mrs. McDaniels was waiting, frantic, on the front sidewalk. "Honey, I'm so sorry! We're both sorry! Daddy called you to apologize. It'll be okay. We'll work it out somehow."

Megan ran up to her, burrowing into Mrs. McDaniels as she had burrowed into Toby earlier.

"Toby, thank you . . . so much. Please come in."

"No," he said. "No thanks. I gotta go."

He waited till the two went inside. Then he walked. To school. To the playground, where he sat on one of the wet swings and started pumping. Pumped as hard as he could. He kept swinging and swinging. Thinking about Slammer and Crusher. About Megan and Mr. and Mrs. McDaniels. About his mother and Doug and Gordon and Skeeter and Leo and Jeremy and Ms. Blankenship. Even Mrs. Hawkins and Mr. Fenning. Almost everyone he knew. On and on he pumped, letting the night rush over him. When his thoughts finally came around to his father, he realized he had thought himself out.

He was halfway home when the Jeep came to a sudden stop a few yards in front of him, then backed up.

"Need a lift?" Doug called out the window. "Your mother's worried. She's home. The party was busted. We got a call from Caruthers. Guess the old man called the police too."

Toby got in. Doug had on a jacket over his Fred Flintstone costume, his legs bare from the knees down. "Did you and Mom win?"

"Win what?"

"The costume thing."

"No. . . . It wasn't all that much fun, really. Too crowded. We'd have been better off staying home."

TWENTY-ONE

Leo was on cloud nine the next day. "Man, I'm sorry you had to miss it," he said. "We played spin the bottle. Josie's mom said it could only be for hugs."

"Was Luanne there?" Toby asked.

Leo made a face. "Yeah. And the bottle stopped at her first. You had to pick someone to go to the laundry room with you. She picked Denny. Can you believe it?"

Toby thought he could believe anything after last night.

"I don't even care," Leo said. "It wasn't in the cards for Luanne and me. But guess who picked me?"

"Leo, just tell me."

"Gina! Gina picked me. And when we went to the laundry room, it was like in the movies—you know, stars and stuff. We hugged for five whole minutes. Then the timer went off. And when we came out, everyone clapped. I'm really sorry you couldn't be there," he said again. "I waited and waited for you. Finally it was only Josie and Melissa and me and Jeremy, and Jeremy's dad dropped me home."

He stopped like it was something Toby would be mad at.

"What did they have to eat?" Toby said.

"Little sandwiches," Leo said. "They weren't that great. And chips and stuff . . . the usual."

"Clam dip?"

"Nope. Bean something or other."

Later, Toby went to see Ms. Blankenship. "Megan is very lucky to have a friend like you," she said.

Toby didn't tell her about Slammer and Crusher.

That night Toby watched some TV, then went to his room to finish his life-story book. The book was due the next day. He had eight pages done, only two to go, but he knew he didn't have to worry.

I don't know why people do dumb things. I don't know why people scare their little girls and make them cry and run away on Halloween, when things are supposed to be happy. Or why some jerk has to pour beer into a fishbowl when the fish never hurt anyone and just want to live their lives and swim and eat and play.

I don't know a lot of things.

The only thing I know for sure is how fast things change. Next year everything will be different from now. Mr. Fitness might be my stepdad. It could happen. Maybe he's not so awful bad. Maybe I'll change in how I feel about him. Anything's possible. Ms. Blankenship says you've got to let the bad stuff run off your back. Otherwise you quack up. But it's not easy. It's not easy having Slammer and Crusher gone.

I never thought I could write so much. That's another thing I didn't know. So I guess you never know everything, even if sometimes you think you do. Because things change. People change. They go away, like Blaine Kellogg. And then people come into your life at weird times, like Megan and Jeremy. And then there are some people you don't know how they're gonna turn out. Like Mom. And Mr. Fitness. And Gordon. Maybe Gordon'll become a decent bald guy someday. I doubt it.

Right now that's my life. Mom says she's gonna find another job so she doesn't have to work nights. She made Gordon quit his grocery job so he wouldn't mess around so much anymore. As for me, I don't think I care that much about being the king of the school anymore. Maybe it's not such a hot job after all. Ms. Blankenship says the real warrior is the guy inside you. She says I acted like a warrior when I went to Megan's house instead of to the party—that I was a warrior when I helped Megan. And Megan thinks I'm pretty okay, I guess. Today I got a letter from her in the school mail. It was a big heart. Inside was a poem that said,

I WISH MY BIKE COULD FLY
SO I COULD RIDE UP IN THE SKY.
I WISH I HAD A BROTHER
AS NICE AS TOBY SCUDDER.

□   □   □

Mr. Fenning called for the books the next day. "It's the moment you've all been waiting for," he said to a chorus of groans. Some kids were scribbling to finish their required ten pages. Toby had written twelve. Maybe a C, he thought.

"Don't forget to put 'Read' or 'Don't Read' on the front," Mr. Fenning said.

It was strange, but Toby almost didn't want to give up his book. "Mr. Fenning, do we get these back?" he said.

"They'll be back to you within a few days," the teacher said. "So if you haven't filled them, you can continue after that."

"I filled *four* books," Veronica said.

"There're plenty more," Mr. Fenning said, opening the cupboard and pointing to a new stack. "Anytime you need another, here they are."

The tip of Toby's pencil had broken off. He took the pencil to the sharpener. "Hey," he said to Jeremy, who was writing full speed.

"Hey," Jeremy said, looking up.

"You probably don't know anything about wrestling, right?"

"Huh?"

"TV wrestling. *Saturday Night's Main Event.*"

"I saw it once," Jeremy said. "I liked the guy that had the big snake in the ring."

Toby gave the sharpener a few quick turns. He took out the pencil, blowing the new point clear of shavings. "That's Jake 'The Snake' Roberts," he said. "The snake's a python, over ten feet long . . . named Lucifer."

"Oh," Jeremy said.

"Sometimes Leo and I do stayovers and make popcorn and watch the matches. It's almost like being there."

"Do I have everybody's book?" Mr. Fenning called.

Returning to his seat, Toby cupped one hand to block the view and wrote *READ* on the cover of his life-story book. He knew Mr. Fenning would be bored with what he'd written, but in the end he decided it would be a waste if no one read it at all.

□　□　□

"You think you'll be moving in with your dad?" Toby asked Leo on the way home from school. He wanted to know. Even if it was bad. Better to know than to be surprised. He'd had enough surprises these last couple of days.

Leo looked like a dragon with glasses, his breath turning steamy in the cold air. "The whole thing's off," he said. "Dad's working graveyard till at least

January. Mom said it'd be a bad idea for me to switch schools halfway in the year."

"You glad?"

"Course I'm glad. It's our year, remember?

"And get this," he added. "I've been working on Dad. He says I might be able to invite you to come with us to California next summer. Can you feature it? Us two on the beach . . . with the binoculars and the babes?"

The wind gusted into Toby's back, whipping his camouflage pants. He had a hard time thinking about California when it was so cold out. He pulled up his jacket collar and was about to say "That'd be great" to Leo when he saw it.

"Look!"

It was snowing. The first snow of the year. Light and fluffy. Not enough to stick, probably. But snowing. Toby caught a snowflake on his tongue. Then another and another.

"Snow!" Leo said, turning his face upward and doing a little dance. "And tomorrow's Saturday!" He stuck out his tongue.

"It tickles," Toby said, the newsflash blipping on.

Mr. Blaine Kellogg, cereal executive and father to one Tobias Michael Scudder, 12, of Vancouver, WA, disappeared today. "Just vanished," his secretary told a crowded courtroom. "Like a snowflake on a tongue."

Contacted by phone, Tobias told reporters he wasn't surprised. "Dad has a tendency to disappear," he said

"Which is too bad, 'cause he's missing a lot. Like Mrs. Hawkins' tradition of TP-ing her own tree. And what Kiddie Pals are. And how Gordon will probably go bald. And how his son, me, Toby Scudder, Ultimate Warrior, wrote twelve whole pages. Front and back."

About the Author

David Gifaldi based much of *Toby Scudder, Ultimate Warrior* on his experiences as a classroom teacher in Vancouver, Washington. Mr. Gifaldi graduated from Duquesne University, in Pittsburgh, with a degree in English. He tutored children and worked as a substitute and full-time elementary school teacher while beginning his writing career. He is the author of many short stories and five books for children, including *Gregory, Maw, and the Mean One*. David Gifaldi and his wife, Marita, live in Portland, Oregon.